THE FOUNTAIN OF YOUTH

ORDER OF THE BLACK SUN - BOOK 15

PRESTON WILLIAM CHILD

HEIKEN MARKETING

PROLOGUE

Latvia – 1938

SHIMMERING *stars from fresh droplets of rain beautified the otherwise vile streets of Riga. It was late, late in so many ways. The war was looming and for the company it was too late to turn back. Even Ami knew it, and she'd been so obsessed with her performance career that not even World War II had been deemed reason enough to take a break. And why should it? At sixteen years of age she was in the prime of her youth and the world awaited her, but even she admitted to feeling somewhat apprehensive about what was coming.*

The reality pressed upon them all, but Ami vowed to do everything in her power to keep the minds of her colleagues off the dangers of touring Europe. In the imminent shadow nearing her Baltic home, they could all feel the hellish breath of the volatile dragon that crawled at the feet of the SS in Germany.

Ami stared out over the almost deathly silent streets, playing witness only to half-hearted solicitations by drunken men and desperate women in the shelter of the night below the Orfeju Opera House. Her ankles ached under her slender frame, something that came only with overexertion or sickness. Either way, it was her secret to keep. Through tear-riddled blue eyes she gazed into the cold night, counting the steeples between her and the shoreline where the ocean lapped gently in invitation.

"Ami, are you coming, dear?" she heard Lamma's soothing voice from behind her. "You cannot occupy the change rooms all night, you know." He neared her in a humorous rendition of some humpback creature, reaching out to capture her, making his voice quiver in mock warning. "You do know that the opera house is dreadfully haunted, don't you? It's not safe for pretty ballerinas to be locked in here at night just because they missed the call time for closing."

"Oh, can it, Lamma," Ami snickered. She adored the fifty-five-year-old company director and his silly attempt at cheering up his troop of young aspiring professionals. "You don't scare me."

He shed his momentary show and stood next to her in his full tallness. "What is so fascinating that you would risk getting locked in here?"

"Honestly, I lost track of the time. There was nothing out there keeping my attention other than the ocean air and thinking about the future of the company," she admitted. "Let me get my coat. I've already changed out of my pointes, see?"

"Well done," he replied dryly. With folded arms he waited for his last performer to finish changing and join the rest of the company downstairs before heading to the lodge.

"I'm going to miss this place. It's quite beautiful," she mused while

running a brush through her lavish, long, blond locks. Rapid scoop-like movements swept her lengthy tresses into a neat bun. She buttoned up her coat as Lamma opened the door for her. It was his subtle way of rushing people along when he was getting impatient.

"It's wonderful, but we can't stay. In two days we dance for the German devils in Denmark. They've taken up residence near the Kongelige Theatre and wish us to entertain them for three nights in a row," Lamma informed her as she passed him.

"You don't sound pleased. They must be paying handsomely, no?" she asked as they ascended the dark wooden staircase that reeked of dust and mold.

"Indeed," he sighed. "And that's the only reason I agreed to the invitation, Ami. To get meals and accommodation free of charge these days is unheard of, as you know."

"Especially for a ballet company like Diaghilev's Ballets Russes," *Ami agreed.*

"What I fear more is the prospect of having to repeat this perfor- mance – and I mean that in more than just metaphor – in Berlin once these tyrants have ignited what we all hope will blow over," he lamented. "But it's the only way for us to make a name and a profit at the same time."

Lamma shrugged as he opened the external door at the landing of the ground floor, letting in the light from the pallid streetlamp. Ami could see the lines on his face more deeply than usual. The director was gravely concerned, but Ami maintained her light- heartedness to relieve the stress of the weighty decisions Lamma has had to make for the good of the troop. Out of courtesy to him she said nothing more on the subject and only replied with a smile and a suggestion.

"*Shall we accost the baker tomorrow for those cinnamon rolls you love so much?*"

O<small>SLO</small> – *early 1945*

A<small>FTER</small> <small>TWO</small> <small>NIGHTS</small> *of exceptional skill on stage and equally grand relations with the high officers of the SS present at the banquet, the* Ballets Russes Company *excelled yet again on the third night. It was an evening arranged especially for the Führer, accompanied by four of his high commissioners in charge of various progressive Nazi endeavors. On short notice, considering the political climate and transport systems, the SS had changed the location of the performances to the Oslo Drama House. It was the pride of the local business chamber organization, which was striving to establish a solid arts program. They wanted to garner support from bigger establishments in and around Scandinavia. Inadvertently, however, it had garnered Nazi support instead.*

"*By now you should be used to it,*" Claire told Ami as they peeked from the dark security of the wing drapes of the theatre.

"*Four months in allied countries and now we're right in the middle of Hitler country?*" Ami replied. "*No, I can't seem to shake this bad feeling.*"

"*Relax. We're dancers—performers, not soldiers. They have no tangle with us. They're just men in scary uniforms,*" Claire told the nervous principal dancer she'd befriended months before.

"*Men in scary uniforms who kill thousands of innocent people – women and children even – as easily as if taking a shit, Claire. They're evil. Just look at them!*" Ami insisted. "*Is that Hitler?*"

Lamma perked up behind the two ballerinas. "That's him. Monster. I wish I could burn this place down during intermission while that son of a whore takes a piss in the men's room."

Ami had never heard Lamma say anything hostile in her life, and she could see that Claire was as surprised as she was. But under the circumstances such utterings were hardly surprising anymore. "Just deliver the same brilliant performance you always do, my darlings. Pretend you are dancing for the gods in some celestial palace," he gestured dreamily. "And once you're done devastating the eyes and hearts of your onlookers with dashing beauty, we'll be out of this city and on our way to Karlstad. Safe."

Claire stared at the SS officers laughing and sipping wine. "Nowhere is safe."

Ami tried her best to un-hear those words, because she absolutely concurred with them. But for now she had to do her best work, not for Hitler, but for Lamma. He had been her mentor and much like a father. He'd trained her to be her best at an early age. Then, he'd taken the company on tour to advance the fame and reputation of his excellent female dancers, herself among them.

"The piano work is a good edge, Lamma," the owner of the building told the director as the ballerinas took the stage in bright competence and astounding flair. "Better than the strings, I think."

"Thank you," Lamma answered, keeping his eyes straight ahead on the ladies on the stage. "We've had to make special considerations for the performances since the war began. All of our male performers have been conscripted, but I couldn't let an already planned tour fall to ruin just because of the German threat to the world, so," he shrugged proudly, "we rewrote the pieces to omit male dancers entirely."

"Not an altogether unpleasant notion to my mind, for one," the

landlord said, smiling as he marveled at the graceful beauty on stage. "But while you were in Britain, you must have had some immense discomfort performing with the Blitz on and all."

"You have no idea, my friend," Lammas sighed, finally facing the Norwegian man he'd once shared a library office with. In London they'd studied Art and Literature together, moonlighting as librarians to supplement their income. "Some nights we'd be getting ready for a performance and just wait for the alarms, positively anticipating the shattering of windows and dying a slow death trapped under a burning beam. It's funny, actually. Here we are behind enemy lines in the very presence of the biggest wolves among them...and it's the safest place in the world!"

Ami's solo piece was due. Lamma was elated to see her flourish flawlessly, as he knew she would. What both disturbed and intrigued him was the way in which Adolf Hitler and his men regarded her. It wasn't so much a look of lust, but their blackened eyes appeared to be savoring her every move, the lines of her body, and how she used it to a point of irresistible allure. They sat just in front of the stage, their banquet table dotted with half-finished dishes on elaborate porcelain plates lined with bottles of the best liquor. Their heads were tilted back in frozen admiration of the stunning young woman adorned in virgin white feather and lace.

For a moment Lamma's eyes met Ami's as she executed a perfect leap, her body in a smooth arch, her front leg kicking upward with astonishing dexterity. Like a swan landing from flight she touched down with little more impact than a feather. With a swift wink at Lamma, Ami prepared for her grand finale, complete with a marvelous set of thirteen fouettés she had mastered months before.

"My God, she is amazing," the landlord smiled again.

"Wait, watch this final spin and tell me she isn't destined for greatness. Without even breaking a sweat Ami executes moves other ballerinas only wish they could." Lamma was boasting like a proud father.

"Are you sure?" the building owner asked, somewhat dampened in his enthusiasm. "She just winced like she is in pain or...uncomfortable?"

"I doubt that," Lamma snapped. His faith in Ami's abilities was unshakable. But that faith was tested a moment later when Ami's ankle gave way during her sixth fouette and snapped like a twig under her meager weight. With the force of her spin her body propelled forward, sending her plummeting from the edge of the stage. Lamma watched as his principal dancer crashed into the glass bottles and plates on the table of the Nazi High Command with an ungodly din that had him certain she'd be executed for it.

The officers jumped up amongst laughter, panic, and sympathy. Collecting the unfortunate Ami's unconscious body, some of the subordinates of the visiting SS called for medics to attend to the injured ballerina.

"Get some proper medical help in here!" Hitler shouted, sending soldiers hastening in all directions. The Nazi leader and two of his men gathered around the girl.

"Fallen swan," one of them said as Lamma rushed to her side. He wasn't sure if it been said, in fact, by the demonic leader himself, but at that moment he couldn't care less. All he cared about was Ami.

Her ankle joint had broken off completely inside her flesh, leaving her foot dangling on purple, swollen tissue. From her fall, her body had sustained severe lacerations and she'd bled her white raiment to crimson.

"The glass has ravaged her body, but her face seems to be unscathed, no?" Lamma said to nobody in particular, wondering if cruel men even heard the words of a good man. "Right?"

The tyrant with the toothbrush moustache stepped in front of Lamma, barring him from the wounded ballerina. Laying his hand on Lamma's shoulder, he looked him straight in the eye and said, "She will stay beautiful. Of that I will make sure."

1

*N*ina took a deep breath, drawing the soothing nicotine from her cigarette down her throat, where it burned delightfully into her chest. She held it there for a moment, before blowing out the weak tuft that remained. On her lips a naughty smile appeared, and her dark eyes stared into space as she partook in her vile rebellion against the spreading cancer that slept in her cells like the secret she had made of it. It wasn't a secret borne out of some hopeful notion that she might defeat the illness without having to burden her friends with the awful truth, nor was it kept from them out of some noble self-pity. Nina merely didn't care anymore.

She still resented Purdue, even though he'd been doing everything in his power to accommodate her need for space from him. She appreciated it to an extent, but she couldn't help but feel that it was his fault that she'd fallen prey to the radiation of Chernobyl's Reactor 4. Apart from this, she'd been gradually growing indignant with his constant excursions, especially his masterful manipulation of Sam and herself to assist in his dangerous pursuits. This just happened to be the last straw. She'd had countless fallings out with Purdue before over always putting her life in danger, but now it was literally causing her a slow death.

The search for the Amber Room had indirectly been to blame for her radiation sickness and subsequent cancer. And the search for the Amber Room was yet another of Purdue's happy perils, in her opinion. As a result, he was at fault for it all.

Sam had no idea that she was sicker than the radiation poisoning, since her cancer exhibited similar signs. He thought she was on the mend, as did Purdue, and she intended to keep them in the dark. Subsequently, she'd become quite indifferent to her condition and elected to carry on as best she could in the same way she always had. After all, there was no need to wither. Her life had been a strong and adventurous journey, and she had attained most of her goals, casting aside those aims that had become redundant, such as being a tenured professor in Edinburgh.

THAT DREAM WAS MEANINGLESS NOW, because Nina had learned so much about the practical application of her knowledge. She realized early on that her knowledge would feel wasted in the dusty lecture halls of small institutions. The notion of wasted knowledge in musty classrooms faded as she extinguished the butt just short of a pile of papers. Nina sighed. Two towers of paper, folders, and cardboard drowned her small frame, flanking her workspace where she was marking term papers.

"Phase two," she groaned as she discarded the dead fag in

the tainted glass ashtray. "Let's see if any of you can cogently explain implications of the First World War hell syndrome on the social structure of welfare systems."

Nina was working under a weak bulb crowned by an old iron cover that was suspended from the ceiling. The beam of light fell almost exclusively on her and her desk, giving the effect of some divine light illuminating Nina's head like a halo. Around her the dark swallowed up everything else, save for the floating dust particles lit up by the bulb.

"Almost done, I see," a female voice chimed from some-where ahead in the dark. "Good God Dr. Gould! You look like the subject of a military interrogation in here."

"Gertrud!" Nina said quickly, but it was too late. The friendly assistant switched on the overhead lights, practi-cally blinding Nina while the pain in her ocular cavities devastated her. "Jesus! What did I tell you about the lights?" Instantly Gertrud killed the lights, having forgotten the special circumstances of the visiting fellow.

"Oh my God, I'm so sorry!" she exclaimed, her right hand barely keeping even enough not to spill the coffee from the cup she was holding.

Nina exhaled and slammed her red biro down on the papers under her hands. "No, Gertie, *I* am sorry. I didn't mean to shout. The light just stings like hell."

"Oh, I'm sure. Of course it does. I feel like a right idiot," the forty-year-old assistant apologized. "But here is a nice cuppa for you, if that could in any way afford me forgiveness."

"Blessings!" Nina replied with a smile, thankful that she had something to wash down the awful dryness in her throat.

She was sitting in the small office adjacent to the library archives of St. Vincent's Academy of History and Science in Hook, Hampshire. It was a modest institution – one of those she'd sworn she would not revert to – in the Hart district, where an old colleague used to teach in the late 90s. When the board of directors decided to change the nature of the establishment a few months before, they'd restructured the faculty to only three permanent lecturers. These they incorporated with several visiting professors and teachers to bring the college more diverse and interesting tutors.

Under the main library building, the Scottish history expert decided to make her home in the deserted chamber of dust and darkness. Not only were her eyes deteriorating and sharp light was out of the question, but she also enjoyed the absolute privacy of the location. It was a welcome change out of the harsh spotlight, not to mention a well-earned break from being in hazardous situations.

"So, how are they doing?" Gertrud asked as her eyes combed the scribbled writing and typed submissions in front of the visiting lecturer.

"Not bad, actually," Nina replied, sipping her coffee. "I think they grasp most of the subject in context, but some of them are entirely too preoccupied with politics in their theses."

"I suppose it's all about influence." Gertrud pursed her lips and shrugged.

"How do you mean?" Nina asked.

"Surprisingly, most of the students at this institution are not from here. In fact, they come from all over England. Many of them are sent here by their families, and those families all have one thing in common…more than just being wealthy land owners, that is."

"Do tell," Nina implored, minding her lips on the scalding beverage.

"Well, I've just always found it peculiar how a lot of them happen to be of German origin – I mean, contemporary German origin. At least as far as the students studying sciences here are concerned. It's not so true of the history students. Why would they bother sending them to a little, godforsaken school in the English countryside if they could be educated by the most prominent universities in Europe, right?"

"I suppose," Nina said. "But perhaps, like me, they just thought it would be less stressful to be away from distractions and better for academic focus to have a more personalized education out here."

"Perhaps. I just think their families have some sort of influence over them to get them to study in avenues they normally wouldn't care much for," Gertrud answered.

"Are these families rooted in politics, then?" Nina asked.

"Most, yes. I could be way off, but I think it could be the reason your students are more politically orientated, you know? Just rapping it off here. I'm not an expert or anything," she chuckled. "Let me leave you to your work. I have some research to finish for Prof. Hartley, anyway."

"Alright," Nina smiled. "Thanks for the lovely coffee!"

Gertrud walked into the brighter light of the landing that led to the stairwell and gave Nina a jovial wave as she vanished around the doorway. Suddenly Nina felt utterly lonely. She chalked it up to the illness spreading through her body, influencing her psyche. She tilted the green mug where her coffee barely filled the bottom.

"Shit," she murmured. A break would be welcome, but she felt reluctant to brave the light and the obligatory greetings and small talk on her way to the kitchen. The thought of fake-smiling and clenching her fists to get through trivialities she was not in the mood for was too much to bear to leave the secluded tomb of her students' clumsy efforts. The dark, once her enemy in the subterranean tunnels of the Ukraine, had now become her ally and she did not want to leave it – not even for coffee.

Eventually her lack of concentration won the joust and Nina stood up to refill her cup. Her chest itched and she scratched, involuntarily igniting a coughing fit that had her rib cage constricting so intensely that she collapsed to her knees. With every expulsion, her back stung as if punctured by a railroad spike and her throat burned from the effort. Much as she tried to keep it down, her coughing came out loudly in the dead silence of the basement area.

When she eventually regained her composure, Nina's eyes were watering profusely. The stabbing pain in back persisted and her chest was still heaving in an effort to catch her breath. The pounding headache that ensued was only worsening and she thought to take a headache pill with her fresh cup.

"Fuck me," she panted, clearing her throat to get her voice back. Her body ached, but she perked up to look as normal as possible when she left the dark, tiny office. Along the steps ran an old wooden balustrade, winding along upward to the ground floor where the stained glass windows shed a plethora of colors at her feet.

Muttering voices came within earshot as Nina tiptoed to the kitchen at the end of the passage. As she drew nearer to where the kettle beckoned, the voices became clearer. Two women were speaking in hushed tones, but Nina's hearing had become exceedingly better since her sight had begun to wane and she could hear the words, though she could not place the subject.

"He's out of his mind if he thinks I'm going run those records for him again," the older lady argued.

"You have to. It's your duty as department head, Christa, to do research for the Dean. This is something important. It was the saving grace of so many children over the years and you owe it to..." the other woman tried to reason, but the first snapped her to silence.

"I owe nothing to the legacy of a bloody Kraut and his twisted regime, Clara! My allegiance is to my husband, not his mother."

Nina had to come in for her coffee, so she pretended to be oblivious to the conversation. Even so, upon sight of her both women fell silent and nodded to her in mock tolerance.

Aye. There it is, that lovely fake amity I've come to love around here, Nina thought to herself as the two women smiled kindly at her.

"Good day, Dr. Gould," Mrs. Clara Rutherford greeted, prompting her colleague with her eyes.

"How are you getting on here at our little establishment,

dear Nina?" Dr. Christa Smith asked, dunking her tea bag into her cup.

"Good afternoon, ladies," Nina said mildly, trying to urge the kettle to boil the water faster than what science allowed. "So far it is very pleasant, thank you."

"I trust you don't find our curriculum too primitive, what with your extensive travels and, well let's just say it, celebrity," Christa said in questionable jest.

Clara lightly slapped her on the hand. "I'm sure Dr. Gould does not appreciate all the unwanted attention, Christa. Am I right, Nina? I'm sure I would loathe all that public attention myself, even if I was responsible for so many successful explorations of historical value."

"Hardly a celebrity, Dr. Smith," Nina said softly. Having done her homework on the establishment before accepting the invitation from Smith as a visiting lecturer, she knew that Clara was Smith's lapdog. She'd never finished her doctorate and thus deemed herself lesser than the charismatic chairperson of St. Vincent's Academy of History and Science.

A warm sensation tickled Nina's upper lip. Both the women in her company gasped. Nina's index finger explored the bottom bend of her nose. When she checked her finger, it yielded a bloody tip.

"Oh, it's just a nosebleed," Clara said.

"Aye," Nina said, wincing as her headache increased to a skull-splitting level, "just a nosebleed."

2

*I*n Edinburgh, Dave Purdue was having a stiff drink on one of his balconies. It was his third in the past ten minutes. He'd been sleeping well enough of late, but the incomplete treatment he'd abandoned when Sam had broken him out of the Sinclair Medical Research Facility was catching up to him. He knew it would be imperative for him to return to the institution eventually, but he was reluctant because of the ambiguous circumstances of his so-called release. Yet his persistent problems with discerning reality prompted him to give institutionalization some serious thought.

"Shall I dish up, sir?" his cook asked from the study doorway.

"Yes, thank you. Just give me a few more minutes," he called back to her. He felt the electric tension of a brewing rainstorm over his mansion and could smell the wondrous mossy scent of dead leaves and moist soil under the giant oaks that cradled Wrichtishousis. It had been his home for what seemed like an eternity, and yet he felt only like a visitor these days. His mind left him sometimes, not in an insane way, but rather it would neglect whatever he'd been trying to quantify or comprehend at that moment and wander off to something else. And that something else would usually constitute something reckless, almost as if it had been implanted by an external force. It had been months since he'd been tortured by the Order of the Black Sun, and his mind still suffered from the onslaught of their brainwashing methods.

"No wonder Nina hates me," he glowered as he emptied the contents of the glass. "But I'm not one to lose my ego over women, am I?"

"Excuse me, sir?" the cook asked.

"Oh, uh, I'm just musing by myself," Purdue chuckled as he skipped over the threshold of his balcony doors and locked them behind him. "Better to keep the storm out."

"Indeed, Mr. Purdue. I hear they are expecting a right Biblical flood for the next two days," she babbled, dishcloth in hand. "But not to fear, the week's groceries have been bought and delivered, so you should be fine cloistered up in here."

"I understand your concern, my dear," Purdue told her as they approached the dining room at the bottom of the stairs, "but I assure you, my sense of adventure is far from doused. I shall be my old self as soon as I finish my research into the stone spheres of New Zealand. Who knows? I might even drag my personal chef with me."

"No, thank you, sir," she protested with a superstitious tone. "I'd rather leave all the chasing after spooky artifacts and strange places to your capable hands. No, thank you."

Purdue grinned in amusement at her repudiation. Sometimes he forgot just how dangerous and unusual his excursions were. He sat down in his large dining room where he liked throwing cocktail parties and private fundraisers, and where he held meetings for the planning of expeditions with his vast array of experts. Only now their voices were absent, their educated speculation lacking, and Purdue felt the overwhelming pressure of the emptiness around him.

The food was exquisite, as usual, but his tongue refused him the pleasure. Loud and persistent, he used his utensils on the fragile plate to keep his mind from realizing that he was alone. Cheer seeped out of him like a draining wine vat as he gradually slipped from control.

"Agatha," he whispered to his deceased sister. "Are you even dead? Am I just a shard of Edgar Alan Poe's *Roderick*, the modern day, stinking rich, super-smart twin brother who buried his sister when she was still alive?"

His stomach contracted, expelling his recently swallowed morsels. Purdue felt his mind fall to shadow, to a place where Klaus Kemper wanted him. Fully aware of the imminent darkness and loss of composure, Purdue jumped up, grabbed a bottle of Jim Beam from his liquor cabinet, and ran for his laboratory. He deposited himself in the second section of his lab, where he kept his audio-visual gadgets and monitors for entertainment and editing purposes when shooting documentaries.

Quickly he placed his headphones over his ears and opened the drive to choose an album to listen to. His blue eyes swam in tears as Klaus Kemper's evil coursed through his brain, still programmed to obey the late tyrant through a numeric-hypnotic method.

"Oh God, no! Not *The Doors*! Not now. Jesus, that's all I need while trying to get out of a mindbender!" he told himself. Quivering over his lips, his breath flowed hot and smelly from the neat gulps of bourbon he'd forced down to keep the commands from holding sway. He'd discovered that Kemper's brainwashing was impeded by alcohol. Every time his mind locked into a sequence of numbers and he felt an urge beyond his control, drinking hard liquor would subdue his reasoning and numb his motor skills, fooling his mind into being too dumbed down to follow the subliminal orders.

"Here we go. Here we go!" Purdue smiled as tears streaked over his face. "That'll do it." His cursor fell on Lightnin' Hopkins and Johnny Cash. Another swig burned right through the tears as the blues took the first turn. Purdue pulled up a chair, adamant to apologize to his cook for the waste of good food. But for now he felt the need to discard anything scientific or sober, trying to save his brain as much as his very soul. He sank back in the chair and relished the sensation of inebriated stupidity while the music closed off his calculative cognition.

"Who is Agatha again?" a man's voice asked outside his mind.

"Don't be stupid. Everyone knows who she is – was," Purdue strained to speak the words while the alcohol infused his body. "She was my sister, but I left her buried under a library full of forbidden information." He chuckled weakly, tears streaming over the edge of his face in droplets. "You know, she'd always wanted to be a librarian."

"Where is this library?" the voice asked once more. "Can you show me on a map?"

"I don't have to," Purdue smiled with his eyes shut tight. The easy melodies of the music meandered over his mind and calmed his body like the bourbon. "I know the coordinates."

"Can you give them to me?" the man asked from the dark that Purdue was reluctant to desert just yet. After all, it was just an alcohol-induced daydream.

"But of course," he told the disembodied voice, unaware of his crumbling consciousness. "It is 45.4408° N...wait....12.31 and then, um, 55° E," Purdue said. A scowl formed. "Or was it South?"

"Let me read that back to you," the man said. "45-44-8," he paused for a moment as if correcting the rest before continuing with, "2-2-58."

Purdue's eyes opened and he found that he was not in the sanctuary of his mansion and was grasping a rolled hand towel where his glass of Jim Beam had been a moment ago. Strapped into a comfortable chair, he noticed a familiar face in front of him.

"Dr. Helberg? We thought you were dead," Purdue marveled.

"No, David. Still kicking," the short man replied, although he'd visibly lost weight since the last time he'd been playing host to Sam, Nina, and a particularly nasty brain-manipulator.

"Good to see you," Purdue nodded.

"David, do you remember what we were just discussing?" the doctor asked him.

"No, I was having a drink in..." Purdue realized that he had never been home in the first place and that familiar sinking feeling hit him again. "Oh, no. No! What did I do this time?"

"Nothing, yet. You were telling me about your sister; that you'd buried her in a library," Dr. Helberg pressed the point of his pen upon the blank line of the notes he kept on his lap, waiting to jot down Purdue's response. He wanted to examine Purdue's recognition patterns after the number sequence. It was all part, literally, of deciphering the numerical structures that activated the subconscious commands in Purdue's brain.

"Oh," Purdue shrugged carelessly, covering up the ugly truth with good acting. "Maybe believing I was inebriated actually transpired in my ramblings. A kind of psychological placebo effect, if you will."

"That's a good hypothesis, David," the doctor smiled, impressed at the notion.

Much as the thought of a contemporary Nazi organization brainwashing powerful financiers appalled him, Dr. Helberg could not help but yield some admiration for the genius behind Klaus Kemper's mental safe lock. The combinations alone were almost impossible to record, let alone how they were programmed into Dave Purdue's head to make him believe that he had, in fact, buried his sister alive. Of course, the good doctor could never admit to it out loud, but Dr. Helberg wished that he could have memorized such a treasury of number combinations to control the minds of others.

What Purdue also hid was the disturbing twinge he felt at the thought of what had just transpired. Now that he had awoken inside being awake, it dawned on him that he could very well be experiencing yet another dimension of reality and not even be aware of it. For all he knew, he was probably still under Reactor 4, running in the dark with Kemper's numbers reprogramming his brain. On the other hand, it had been some time since he'd experienced that familiar involuntary servitude, so maybe this was the *real* reality after all.

"You are doing exceptionally well, David," Dr. Helberg remarked as he ticked off some check boxes on the clipboard he'd retrieved from his case. "I'd venture to say that your problem might well be resolved by next session. The fact that you have exhibited signs of articulate reasoning during these so-called commands says it all. I think the reversal should be completed by Thursday." The jovial doctor smiled as he signed off on the session and released Purdue from his mild restraints to the chair.

"Dr. Helberg, would you do me a favor and drop a line to Albert for me?" Purdue implored, rubbing his wrists to alleviate the chafing.

"Sure," he replied. "Albert..."

"Albert Ashton, a friend of mine. I need him to bring me my Halifax 552, but not the 4788. Okay?" Purdue impressed on the doctor.

"Okay, I'll tell him," he told Purdue somewhat absent-mindedly and packed up his stuff.

"You don't know Albert, do you, doctor?" Purdue said victoriously. "Because, with the number sequence I just gave you, you'd have been compelled to run to the window and check who was following you."

Perplexed, Dr. Helberg stared at Purdue. "What on earth do you mean? Of course I know Albert Ashton. He was...a patient."

"And, oddly enough, you already have the means to override numeric mind control after you investigated the files on Sam Cleave's previous malady, proving that you are not only a charlatan, but one with a dangerous agenda at that," Purdue revealed, taking careful note of the man's facial expression.

The man was trying too hard to appear indifferent, and Purdue noticed that he was dipping his right hand into the case while maintaining eye contact, a blatant betrayal of attempted misdirection. Purdue knew what that meant. He leapt forward to grab the gun that emerged in the fake doctor's hand. Moments later the tall patient and the impostor clashed, falling to the ground in a struggle for the Colt six shooter between their bodies.

The doctor's case tipped over and spilled its contents onto the polished floor where the men were grappling wildly. Pastel folders with various names and notes were strewn in disarray next to Purdue and his assailant. Moments later, two thundering shots clapped and blood spattered brightly on the pale colors of the medical files.

3

*O*rderlies came rushing into David Purdue's room at the Sinclair Medical Facility, examining the corners of the room to check for more attackers. But they soon found that it had been just the one. His body was limp and heavy, smothering the barely conscious Purdue underneath.

"Get him off! Get him off!" the head nurse shouted to the men. "Mr. Purdue? Mr. Purdue, can you hear me?" He sank to his knees beside Purdue to check his vitals, knees in the blood on the floor.

"Mr. Mills, aren't you disturbing a crime scene or something?" a fresh employee asked from the vicinity of the cupboard where the impostor's case had been sitting before the scuffle.

"Why don't you just do as you're told until I've determined if there even is a crime scene? By the looks of these two unconscious, but breathing individuals, it is safe to assume there has been no murder committed, Harold," the veteran medical technician sneered at the rookie. "Yet."

"Yes, sir. What about the weapon, sir?" he dared ask Mr. Mills after his reprimand.

Mills winced irately, but kept his cool. "I'll take care of it, Harold. You just help Jimmy lift Dr. Helberg onto the gurney so that we can get them both to Hopkins Memorial as quickly as possible."

"Yes, sir."

Jeremy Mills surveyed the scene swiftly. He'd had to wait for the police to arrive and stood guard over the room in the meantime. Even without a death, this was a case of attempted murder, or grievous bodily harm in the very least. But Dr. Helberg had to receive immediate medical care due to a gunshot wound to the abdomen and a flesh wound that had ripped through his left oblique. Purdue had been knocked unconscious just as the shot went off when his head had slammed against the cabinet corner during the altercation.

Mills had no idea why this had happened, even less of an idea which of the two men were at fault. Naturally, one would assume that the patient was the instigator, but patients did not keep guns in their rooms, which put the suspicion squarely on the psychologist.

But what disturbed everyone on the staff a few hours later, was that the CCTV footage of the session had not been recorded at all. The oddity was that the security control room had the cameras running at all hours of the day and night, yet during this particular session, the camera had been disabled.

"Pity we don't have a camera in the actual security control room," Mills noted when the police asked for access to the section.

"That is rather ironic, don't you reckon?" the head investigating officer asked snidely. "Where are the patients now?"

"Only one registered patient. David Purdue, Lieutenant," the security officer clarified. "The other is a therapist."

The lieutenant looked at his black book, biting his pen between his teeth as he paged for what he was looking for. "But my information says that Dr. Helberg died a few months ago in a shooting at his practice for which his receptionist was responsible. Therefore, this therapist could not have been the real Dr. Helberg."

At this point the acting administrative head, Melissa Argyle, entered the security room. Her blond hair was visible from under the edge of her knitted beret and lashed out in a halo about her shoulders. Rolling over her fingers was a shiny gilded pen that looked expensive to the investigators.

"We used to have a camera in here too, but it was fried during the last thunderstorm. The company that installed that one was supposed to show up three days ago to install a new one," she explained.

"That makes our job so much harder," the lieutenant from the local precinct muttered as he examined the blackened paint around the wall cable of the device. "Yes, I see here. The wiring has been melted into the casing. Was there any other electrical damage from the same storm? Leakage, structural damage?"

"I don't think so," she replied hesitantly. Melissa was not

sure what he was driving at, but then again, she was just an administrator and pre-grad student of Psychology and with that, a bit naïve. "Why do you ask? What does that have to do with the case?"

"Quite a bit. If other parts of the building were as vulnerable to water damage or electrical failure, it would dismiss the possibility of sabotage," he clarified.

"Sabotage? That's absurd!" she gasped.

"Lieutenant Campbell," a police officer called from under the corner desk where he was following the power points.

"Yes? Do you have something?" Campbell asked zealously.

"I could be mistaken, but it looks like several plug points in this office have been tampered with." The officer's voice was strained as he forced his slightly out-of-shape physique to crouch down lower under the table.

"Here?" Campbell asked.

"All three sockets that could have been used as auxiliary power have been disrupted, sir. Not just that one and not just the wall cable." In turn, Lieutenant Campbell simply gave Melissa and her security officers a good old *I-told-you-so* look and said, "Sabotage."

Melissa folded her arms as a look of worry crossed her face. "So, what do we do now?"

"Now, I shall need all the personnel files on the staff here at Sinclair so that we can run background checks and look for any criminal records. Fortunately for me, you are just the right person to furnish me with that documentation," he said, smiling triumphantly.

He never admitted it, but Campbell loved the fact that he could remind pretty young women that their control was all a dream when matters crossed his turf. The look of discomfort on the barely qualified administrator was a pleasure to behold.

For the rest of the day Campbell annexed the administrative wing, taking up residence in Melissa's office to go through the human resource folders one by one, meticulously checking each individual for a possible motive to be involved in the attempted assassination of a patient.

"See?" Melissa sighed at the wrong end of eleven hours, sitting across from the investigator with the Earl Grey fetish. "Not one of these people have criminal backgrounds, Lieutenant Campbell. That leaves you with nothing on motive; just that the fried circuit was a trick of bad weather and not some premeditated sabotage. What do we do now?"

The police officer had to concede. He had no reason to believe that anyone on the staff had some nefarious associations, although he was familiar with the patient in question and the man's reckless relic hunting.

"Now, Miss Argyle, we have to uncover the real motive for someone to impersonate a deceased psychiatrist...or psychologist, whatever," he told the exhausted young administrator. "I know a lot about Mr. Purdue. In the past he's had some run-ins with the law, but mostly as a trespasser with a penchant for digging in the wrong tombs, if you know what I mean."

"As do I. Mr. Purdue has done a lot for educational institutions the world over, including my own, where he instituted bursaries and shared programs to help the less financially able students. I cannot imagine that someone would want to kill him," she contested naively. And naïve is precisely the unfortunate tone the investigative officer decided not to respond to.

"I suppose it's time for me to leave. We'll be in touch with your legal department about the *negligence* of this facility," he stated deliberately just to watch her squirm at the threat.

"Lieutenant, I have to appeal to your sensitivity here. There's no need to demonize this institution or its staff for a coincidental camera failure that just happened to precede an attack on the premises," Melissa implored, wringing her hands nervously.

"My dear Miss Argyle, I appreciate your point," he replied as he pulled on his coat and sucked up the last bit of cold tea in the latest cup, "but unfortunately, sensitivity is not a virtue I was blessed with."

He gathered up the copies he'd had printed of all the pivotal human resource material and gave Melissa a wink. "We'll be having a chat with Mr. Purdue tonight at the precinct. He was kind enough to agree to an interview with the captain. Thank you so much for all your help. Goodbye." Campbell forced a smile as his eyes quickly fell on Melissa's pen.

"Goodbye, Lieutenant Campbell," she choked out nervously as he left the office.

Peering around her doorway, she watched Campbell traversing the lobby and signing out, before disappearing into the night outside.

"Unbe-fucking-lievable," her full lips mouthed. The sound of her pen tapping against her hip hastened in cadence as her mind raced. "What could Mr. Purdue ever help him find?"

She shook her head and returned to her upturned office to tidy up before leaving for home.

Mills had overseen the cleaning up of the room as two of the janitors returned the place to its former clean comfort after the forensics team had finished with it. He'd left an hour prior to the tenacious detective, but thus was the encumbrance of Melissa's higher paying position that she had to stay later. Sometimes her responsibilities held her captive from any sort of social engagements or the few hours after work where she could wind down from her day.

Peeking through the blinds of her office to see if any staff members were within earshot, Melissa Argyle surveyed the adjacent offices to make sure that she was the only administrative staff member still there. With a deep sigh she picked up her landline and punched in the phone number she knew by heart.

"Guterman, it's me," she said as quietly as she could. "Purdue is aware of the changeling." She paused and swallowed hard before forcing the next report. "And the changeling is under police supervision at Hopkins Memorial." Her eyes caught movement outside her office, but the figure passed by without stopping. She continued listening for more instructions. "Two gunshot wounds. His findings... are in the possession of Lieutenant Campbell at the Dundee Precinct."

The voice on the other end was telling her to be as helpful to the police as possible without betraying the true nature of the situation. She should not draw attention. Then the call was ended unceremoniously.

A loud bang startled her momentarily before Melissa realized that it was the door to the restrooms, the only door in the building that didn't have a fire door closer to ease it shut. "That's another thing I have to get fixed. Geez," she said to herself.

Melissa grabbed her car keys and bag, electing not to wear her raincoat, as the cool night air would be good for her fevered nerves. In the deserted wing of Sinclair, the white luminescent lights hummed over towers of paperwork and dead fax machines. Computer monitors with black screens rested on unoccupied desks, leaving Melissa feeling dreadfully melancholy. Her only company was the second arm on the wall clock ticking monotonously while she locked her door. Her keys fell to the floor when she misjudged the slot and she bent down to pick them up.

From a distance, one of the night janitors watched her grunt from the effort and came to help her.

"Oh my God, you frightened me!" she exclaimed as he rushed to pick up her key for her. "Do you want to give me a heart attack?"

"I'm sorry, Miss Argyle," he apologized, scooping up the keys for the lovely young woman. "Here."

"Thank you," she smiled reluctantly, trying to hide her frustration. But he could see it in her face and manner as she briskly walked off without saying goodbye. His colleague joined him, both men staring at the fresh beauty with the bouncy locks.

"I wouldn't mind test driving that one, hey?" he told his colleague, but the man who'd helped Melissa had a look of distaste on his face when he replied, "You can have her. In bed I like limber women and that kitten is so stiff-limbed she can't even touch her toes."

Laughing, the janitors left the offices to have a smoke outside in the cold where Invergowrie Bay breathed under the full moon.

4

*W*hile Nina was visiting St. Vincent's Academy she resided in the North Hostel, a small assemblage of garden flats on the northern side of the property. The other cottages were not occupied this time of year, as most of the current faculty consisted of permanent teachers and she was the only visiting fellow. Much as she enjoyed the good meals the Dean's mother brought her every night, Nina felt sorry for the elderly lady. She had to work hard not just to cook, but also to walk up the steep lawn every evening to bring Nina her meal.

Even after the historian offered to retrieve her own food, she was politely denied. Tonight she was standing outside, smoking a B&H Silver. The fact that cancer was ravaging her lungs had little effect on the way in which Nina lived her life, as long as the pain was kept to a minimum and the nausea was not overbearing. Having made peace with the state of her health in no way meant that she had made peace with the man she blamed for contracting the disease.

Nina tolerated Purdue only because he'd made some effort

to make up for almost killing her. Other than that, she was not about to start her biological penance a few years too late because of some absurd hope to recover. That ship had sailed, she knew. Keeping the illness from her friends was easy after she'd redirected her medical bills to be charged to her own account instead of Purdue's. All panels and treatment were billed under Dr. Nina Gould, because, as she told the accounts department, it was nobody's business but her own now.

Frigid whips of wind brightened the orange glow of her cigarette, as her dark hair impaired her view of the sleepy streets just off campus. Deep inside Nina there flowed genuine tranquility, even in the volatile forests of uncertainty and fear. She missed Sam and Bruich. The journalist was out on assignment for a government exposé on the Faroe Islands concerning anti-whaling terrorism.

Where his beloved big ginger cat was, however, she had no idea. Sam sometimes left Bruich with her when he had to go somewhere far somewhat quickly, but it had been a while since she'd been chosen to babysit. Bruichladdich always calmed her with his lazy, low-toned meows and his wise cat eyes. He was a wonderful companion – he took care of his own shit, so to speak. Moreover, Bruich reminded her in a silent way that she should not take life too seriously. Right now, she reckoned that big feline would have cheered up her substantially.

From the edge of the garden a black figure emerged. Nina quickly flicked her fag into the pond just off the flower box and watched the water swallow up the tiny puff of smoke it died with.

"Hello, Dr. Gould!" the figure cried through the hard

whisper of the gust. Nina visibly exhaled in relief.

"Mrs. Patterson, I thought you weren't coming tonight," Nina replied as she met the old lady halfway. "Let me take the tray. I can't believe you're coming out in this cold weather just for me."

The elderly woman gave her a kind smile as she passed Nina the tray. "Och, deary. It's not just for you." Her glimmering eyes held some arcane message behind the words she spoke, but Nina was not sure if it was worth asking about. The smell of the food was irresistible and it was only when Nina caught a whiff of the dumplings and stew that she had to admit how hungry she actually was.

"You're too kind," Nina told Mrs. Patterson when she'd put the tray on the table. "Please come in."

"I can't stay for long," the old woman said as she did every time Nina attempted to have a proper conversation with her. "So sorry I'm late tonight..." she said and then hushed her tone as she leaned in to share what was probably blasphemy around here, "but there was a bit of a squabble at home tonight and I had to resolve that first before coming over."

"Oh my goodness! I hope it wasn't too serious?" Nina answered as she removed the cling wrap with as much grace as a ravenously hungry woman could.

Mrs. Patterson just shrugged, "Och well, you know, the cattiness of women often cause confrontation and the men usually don't know how to avert the catfights. I just take them with a pinch, you know, but sometimes you just have to say something. And I said something."

"The Dean's wife?" Nina assumed in a lighter tone.

"How could you tell?" the astute Mrs. Patterson replied with a laugh.

"Aye, I knew I wasn't the only one to find Christa a bit..." Nina tried to think of a nice word, but it took her too long.

"Bitch?" Mrs. Patterson asked sincerely. "Blind people can see that. Deaf people can hear that. Old people can affirm that."

The latter statement was a bit off the former, but Nina chalked it up to an old lady's idiosyncrasy. Suddenly Mrs. Patterson looked at her watch. A look of what could very well be panic crossed her face as she looked up from it, her dark eyes peering into Nina's. There was no denying that Mrs. Patterson wished to share something with Nina, but an unspoken urgency had her wavering.

"What is it, Mrs. Patterson?" Nina asked as she eyed the dumplings. On one hand, she wished the old woman would leave so that she could eat already. But on the other, the Dean's mother seemed truly pressed to tell her something that Nina would want to know.

"You had a nosebleed today, I hear? Are you alright?" the old lady asked Nina, still keeping her voice down.

"Oh, that? That was nothing," Nina fibbed to remove all concerns, but she did not realize what Mrs. Patterson was aiming at. "Just too long under the floor with those examinations, I suppose. Not a big deal."

"You smoke?" Mrs. Patterson asked, quickly leaning back to check the lawn in between words.

"Aye? That is my prerogative," Nina snapped a little. She was in no mood for yet another lecture on her health and the obvious, done-to-death sermons on smoking. On top of that, she wasn't going to give up smoking just because smoking was prohibited in the cottages.

"Yes, it is," Mrs. Patterson agreed. "You keep smoking, alright? Keep to what makes you happy. We all have vices and I believe even the deadly ones are worth the pleasure."

Is this reverse psychology? Nina wondered. It was such an unusual response to get from the Dean's mother.

"Um, thank you?" Nina smiled amusedly. Mrs. Patterson returned her smile, but it swam in apprehension. "I have to go, Dr. Gould. Just you...you keep on doing what you..." she started walking out the door, trying not to cry.

"Mrs. Patterson?" Nina said, feeling that something really amiss, but the woman just kept moving on to return home. She kept looking back at Nina with some desperate affirmation.

"We don't realize how little time we have, Nina. Enjoy every moment, every bad habit, because before you know it, your youth is gone with your strength and then you will regret all the things you did not relish, my dear," she crossed onto the lawn. "Goodnight, my dear."

Nina frowned, dumplings in hand and very confused. "Goodnight, Mrs. Patterson."

With her appetite somewhat dampened by the strange conversation she'd with Mrs. Patterson, Nina wolfed down the dumplings one by one. She couldn't finish all of the stew, though, as it ignited the lurking nausea inside her. Every so often Nina would be reminded that she was sick and this was one of those occasions. Her stubborn nature did not afford her the luxury of acceptance or hope, and therefore the waning historian kept living in denial of her deteriorating state.

When she'd eaten her fill and successfully suppressed the night's impending vomiting session, she stepped outside for another fag. It must have been Mrs. Patterson's mention of the domestic ructions that made it clearer, but Nina noticed that the lights were still on at the Dean's residence about three hundred meters from her cottage. With her ears now tuned to the argument, she could hear the vague sounds of heated voices coming from inside the large house.

"No wonder they're fighting, with that bitch Christa living there," Nina scoffed as she drew the smoke deeper in, deeper than she usually did, deep enough to constitute deliberate harm. But this time she got more than she bargained for. As if her fading body were retaliating, her lungs convulsed in a coughing fit. She felt like an amateur smoker – she was coughing just like had when she'd started at the age of sixteen after Jimmy Harrison dumped her.

Finally Nina's attack subsided, leaving her weeping in pain. The cigarette had fallen from her fingers and it rolled rapidly toward the edge of the steps that led down to the lawn. Against the wall outside her front door she leaned hard against the coarse paint while clutching her chest, but it was her back that was on fire. The region underneath her right scapula especially seemed to tear from the surrounding tissue every time she coughed, and it stung so badly that she cursed through her tears.

But what followed was a nightmare for Nina Gould. From the crying spell she sank to her haunches, burying her hands in her hair, trying not to draw her breath too deeply.

Her scalp felt loose, in a way, when she lifted her head and her hands fell to her knees.

"Oh Jesus!" she cried. "No, no, no! Oh Jesus, no!" she mumbled insanely as tufts of hair stayed behind in her palms. The pain in her back was suddenly not her worst agony, as she felt around her head only to discover that her hair had started falling out. In disbelief, Nina looked at the result of even the gentlest run of her fingertips over her hair. "Christ, no!" she kept repeating from a whisper to the crescendo of her emotions where she screamed hysterically into the cushion on the sofa inside.

She knew it was true. She knew she had to expect this sooner or later, but now that it had actually happened for real, she couldn't deal with the shock. Nina refused to believe what she knew was real. There was no denying the clumps of hair in her hands. For the past two weeks she'd been shedding more than the usual amount of hair when she brushed her tresses, but she'd chosen to ignore the obvious portent.

Muffled in the cushion, the sobs of the historian would never be heard through the noisy gales outside. Yet her frantic wails of despair were deafening inside her and around her, the final clout of reality too much to bear. Maybe she should have told Sam, or even Purdue. Maybe she should've counted on their support before she deciding selfishly to exacerbate her condition out of some kind of spite toward the cruel deities that punished her. But now the hour for such things was late. The small fraction of treatment she'd allowed, or could afford, was now depleted and she was on her own in every way.

Nina had never been so alone.

5

*K*irkwall, the sleepy Scottish town on the Orkney Islands, was suffering a terrible storm that, according to the weather station, threatened to remain indefinitely. Just a few kilometers from the Bay of Weyland, the exclusive clinic, owned by Purdue's holding company, had their generators on to brave the power outage. Power cuts had been plaguing the town since the night before, two days into the unexpected tempest that had approached from the northeast over Everbay and clean across Balfour.

The townspeople had had little warning, but they managed well enough with what they had. They knew to stay indoors while the rain pelted the landscape. Unfortunately for some of them, like Evelyn Moore, work was far too important for the greater good. She still had to commute from the western region to the clinic, where she served as an accounts administrator. The highly qualified accountant-come-business executive had been employed by David Purdue since 2011. By doubling her salary and including a nice townhouse in

Kirkwall, he'd effectively lured her away from her old job in London. And Evelyn did not regret it for a second.

At the clinic she was allowed, even encouraged, to work the financial administration of the establishment in the best way she saw fit. Not only was this good for her, but the teams of specialists, scientists, and medical staff she was fortunate to work with made her job more than a living. They were a close-knit family at the clinic, not only because of their pleasant personalities, but because they all shared the same confidence.

Under the ownership and management of Scorpio Majorus, an affiliate of the mighty Brigade Apostate, all staff members at the Orkney Institute of Science were contractually bound by a non-disclosure agreement. Because of the privileged capacity of the research and patients admitted, all personnel were to keep their work to the confines of the clinic perimeter. With the generous benefits supplied by the holding company, the agreement was not difficult to maintain.

Evelyn had had stressful situations, naturally, but all in all she was working her dream job with a group of people she could trust with her life – in every way. The rain had continued even with reports that it could diminish slightly, and Evelyn was already late for work. Moats of muddy water had blocked her way out of the garage this morning. It had taken her over twenty minutes to get her car out of the garage and successfully locked up before she could leave for work.

With her dark hair in soaking disarray and her make-up hideously un-made by the downpour, Evelyn was cussing under her breath as she drove through the grayed-out vernacular-styled houses. She knew full well that speeding even a tad over the limit here could cause almost certain trouble, but she had a meeting with a prominent member of the board and couldn't afford to be late.

Her VW Polo took to the road with little effort and she was grateful for the new tires she'd put on the month before, even though it had cost her a lot in one go. Times like these were why she'd had the new treads fitted, gripping the road under the wet onslaught of the rain. Nervously she clutched the wheel past the giant structure of St. Magnus Cathedral, but she had to admit that she was relieved most people had elected to stay home today. Thanks to them the road was even emptier than the small population usually took up.

After some annoyingly slow crawling due to traffic lights and children's crossings, Evelyn was freed from the grid-like navigation of town and could speed up a bit on the country road towards the clinic. Carness Road wound in obscured turns through the fog and low-hanging clouds.

"Finally!" she sighed, and dared to push the accelerator deeper than usual, vowing to herself to hold the steering wheel extra tightly for the speed she was going. Her wind-shield wipers worked at optimal speed to clear her view ahead as she sped up, leaving the houses, churches, and stops behind. To her left the ocean camouflaged itself by turning the same gray as the clouds that covered it, and to her right there was only flat green country as far as her eyes could survey.

Fifteen minutes after she'd shaken off the more constrained parts of her journey, she finally came to the turn-off toward the clinic. While stationary at the T-junction, Evelyn checked her watch. "Oh shit! Shit!" she moaned out loud. The face of her watch declared that she was, in fact, now three minutes late for work. That meant three minutes late for her important appointment. Without wasting another moment, she turned into the small road and sped forward.

"Thank God it's raining! No tractors. No insane farmers or delivery trucks. Oh God, if I'm not there before him I'm going to lose the contract!" she whined, still trying to fix her drying tresses into something respectable as she chased the end of the road. Evelyn was right. On days like these, the farmers did not bother to check their fields. It was simply too perilous in such hazardous conditions.

Thunder raged above her miniscule vehicle as she approached the last turn-off, but Evelyn could only think of her business with the board member. Far ahead, she could see a slow moving vehicle emerge from the ghostly road. Gradually it turned darker as she drew closer and slowed down against her will.

"Oh, for fuck's sake!" she exclaimed, vexed at the slow manner in which one farmer chose to pull his tractor across the last stretch of road. "I'm late, you idiot!" she shouted and slammed her hand on the wheel. Gearing to second, she released her clutch and checked the opposite lane one more time before accelerating. She passed the melancholy farmer with ease, looking back at him in the rear view mirror with no small measure of annoyance. He was motioning something, but Evelyn had no time to entertain the attitude of a country dweller.

"Oh yeah? Well, screw you too, Farmer Brown!" she cried, as he grew smaller in her mirror.

It was ten minutes past her meeting with the board member and Evelyn dreaded being dismissed. Mr. Purdue did not tolerate inefficient staff and he would have no qualms with firing her on the spot. Evelyn was so concerned about the future of her career that she never saw the small brown hare that sprinted across the roadway until she was right up on it.

"Oh shit!" she screamed and swerved to a hard right to avoid hitting the furry thing.

Her brakes locked and sent her vehicle skidding along for the next few meters, leaving Evelyn no control of the car as she watched the ditch on the side of the road swallow the bonnet. Screaming helplessly, she braced herself subconsciously, but it was no match for the impact as the node of the car buried itself in the thick muddy turf off the road. The accountant's body came to a sudden halt, which broke her ribs and instantly rendered her unconscious when her head slammed against the dashboard between the steering wheel and the driver door.

"DID YOU HEAR?" the filing clerk whispered harshly when she entered the office of Doris Hipman, the administrative manager at the Orkney Institute of Science.

"Hear what?" Doris asked as she unpacked her case and switched on her laptop.

"This morning Evelyn was in a car accident! She's at the town hospital now...in a coma," the middle-aged lady told Doris. "They say she broke five ribs, fractured her skull, and her back was severely injured in the crash."

"Oh my God!" Doris gasped. "I've been calling her incessantly since 8 a.m. because she missed a meeting with one of the main board members!" She rose from her seat and took off her glasses. "When did you get the news?"

"A few moments ago. Dr. Cait told me he got a call from Balfour Hospital. A farmer out on Work Farm was driving behind her when it happened. He said she passed him on the road and he tried to warn her about a broken fence letting animals onto the road," the clerk recounted.

"She hit a sheep or something?" Doris asked.

"Dr. Cait said that apparently she'd swerved for something running out in front of her car and that was when she went off that deep ditch where the fence runs. The road was, of course, too wet when she tried to brake and, well," she shrugged.

"Alright, thanks for informing me, love. I will give Dr. Cait a call and see if we can send her a bouquet this morning, if any delivery vans are willing to go out in this unholy shower," Doris said. When the clerk had left the office, Doris quickly gulped down her tea. With a labored sigh she shook her head and whispered, "Looks like I will have to do the month end accounts as well. Great."

A few hours into the day, after Doris and the other personnel had sent their colleague some flowers, she finished her daily admin duties to handle the first wave of incomplete accounts to be sent out. She knew the basics and had used Pastel and such before, but Doris did not have a personal relationship with the debtors like Evelyn did. After all, it wasn't her job.

But at the institute they all helped out where they could and sometimes took on other duties above their own when needed. So today Doris would play accounts lady as well. By the fourth or fifth record she was becoming more familiar with the statements, businesses, and patients to be directed to. In fact, by 3:48 p.m. Doris Hipman was feeling quite confident that she could easily do Evelyn's job if she ever had to again.

Some of the documents had footnotes scribbled in about the main member responsible for payment, or alternative payment methods for special patients. Little things that only Evelyn knew about, however, did not appear on all the statement records and the latter was the case on the Purdue account of a few months ago, still outstanding by three installments.

"Odd," Doris frowned. "Purdue?"

Upon requesting that the clerk pull the hard copy to make sure, she still found the discrepancy strange. "Why on earth would David Purdue have to pay anything in installments?" she asked the clerk.

"Why not?" the clerk shrugged innocently, provoking Doris' impatience. The acting accountant pushed out her hip and tilted her head with an annoyed sigh.

"Jessica, David Purdue can buy a small country's cash...with his wallet contents at any given moment. The only thing he ever pays in installments is God's salary! This doesn't make sense at all. He could have paid this treatment off in one swoop." She frowned.

"Who is the patient? Is it for his own treatment?" the clerk asked.

"Um, hang on," Doris replied, keen to see what the clerk had brought to her attention. Her eyes rapidly perused the schedules, scripts, and hospitalization duration before she found the patient's name. "Dr. Nina Gould."

"Ah! Yes, that lady was discharged by Dr. Cait just before that historical peace treaty was signed last year," the clerk exclaimed, her face lighting up at the realization.

"What was she in for?" Doris asked, scanning the incomprehensible medical jargon on the sheets. The clerk did not want to exhibit an insubordinate attitude, but it was something that was bound to be written on the very document her superior was holding.

"Uh, I think it should be written..." she said slowly to sound uncertain long enough for Doris to grasp the concept.

"Oh, wait, here it is," Doris exclaimed, leaving the poor clerk relieved that she did not have to point out to Doris how thick she was being. "Treatment for acute radiation sickness," Doris read, and then her voice dampened slightly at the bad end, "and subsequent small cell lung cancer." She looked up through her glasses. "I'll send this one out first. Just in case she needs more consultations."

6

*S*am was crouching on the floor of the ferry, packing his satchel. He'd decided not to keep his long lens Canon around his neck on account of the vile sea spray that could edge into the camera's innards. Around him the bottom parts of passengers' legs moved about as the ferry crossed the icy ocean between the island of Suðuroy, one of the islands of the Faroese archipelago, and the Shetland Islands where he would book a Cessna back to Edinburgh.

"You take pictures of the fjords with that monster?" someone asked him, but Sam was still laboring to get his gear to fit inside the bag without stripping the zippers. His greasy, thick, black hair was wet with saline water, the ends of his locks bending on his tan-colored collar as he moved. As he finally managed to get the last zipper closed, he looked up at the patient man staring down at him.

"Not so much the fjords as the monuments," Sam answered genially.

"Oh, the old churches?" the man asked, his own long blond hair taken back in a low-tied, rough ponytail.

"Also, no. I was up at Eggjarnar for the day to get a view from up there and take pictures of the ruins," Sam told him. He could not help but be intrigued with the Nordic charm of the well-spoken local with the modestly braided beard and ice gray eyes.

"I see. You came all the way from what I guess to be Scotland to take a picture of the old station in Eggjarnar?" The curious man smiled with a cynical wink.

"Only after I did an exposé on the Grind in Hvalba," Sam admitted.

The Nordic man kept smiling, but it became more of a wince at Sam's revelation. "So you're another Sea Shephard lunatic playing judge over thousands of years of tradition for the people here?"

"I'm a journalist who came to get *real* information on the whale hunt, and I've spoken to many native citizens here, sir. True reporting does not include having a predisposed opinion. I report on the origins of matters and events," Sam informed him, trying to keep from sounding defensive. "All I was doing here was getting the real reasons behind the hunt from the actual people who live here, not some outlandish speculation," Sam explained as he leaned on the barrier, subjecting his face and hair to more frigid spray as the ferry sailed on through the grey above and beneath.

"That's a good rule of thumb, my friend," the man nodded satisfactorily, his head turned to survey the waves and what he knew lived within them. "It's good to ask the truth from only those who live it. That's something I can respect, even in enemies. There's something to be said for informed opponents that is far more worthy of respect than ignorant compliance from allies."

"Did you grow up here?" Sam asked, itching to whip out his Panasonic and record the attractive local. "If I may say so, your command of English is exceptional, even with the accent."

"Thank you," the man replied modestly. "I'm from Toftir, on Eysturoy, but I travel extensively all over the world with my various ventures. My command of your language comes from my love for linguistics."

"That's interesting." Sam smiled genuinely. What he found most peculiar about the man was that he could not tell his age. As far as Sam was concerned, the local could have been anything between twenty-eight and fifty-four, as he displayed signs of a number of different age groups altogether. It struck Sam that he was looking at an ancient young man, if there were any such glorious blasphemy in this world by science or God. "So you know what those ruins up there used to be, I would venture to guess."

"I do. It was built up there by the Allies during World War II," he said nonchalantly, tapping his fingers on his windbreaker cuffs. His fingers were decorated with Norse runes, which wasn't unusual, given the countries they were travelling between. But the man's answer hooked Sam.

"What exactly did they do up that high?" Sam pressed.

"They built a Loran-C station. You know, a radio signal to guide British ships and aircraft after the Germans occupied Denmark. The Allies occupied us and used the altitude of the island peaks to their favor," the local explained with articulate precision.

"So that was why there was a bunker and a gun pit up there too!" Sam smiled. "I had some idea of what it was, but I didn't know the details of the story. You should be a guide for the meek tourists who come to take pictures with absent attention."

"I think so, right?" The man laughed with Sam. "But not all tourists are as tolerant and interested in learning, believe me. Throughout the years we've had many wars here, not just the ones you read in history books. Most people make assumptions about a place and treat the people accordingly. But we are storytellers, fathers, chieftains, warriors, fishermen."

Sam was captivated by the serenity of the well-informed and obviously educated local, and he wished he had more time to chat over a whisky or take in a trip on a fishing trawler to find out more about the recent history of this archipelago west of the Norwegian Sea.

"Where are you headed, by the way?" Sam asked. "I would like to pick your brain some more over a drink or two."

"I'm just accompanying a friend of mine, the guy who owns this ferry. He asked if I would tag along today while he made his last trip for the week, so I agreed. Had nothing to do for a change, you know?"

"Wait, you're going back?" Sam asked.

"Going to Sumba to pick up some gear we have to move," the man shrugged. "Why don't you stay one more day, then…?"

"Oh, shit, my manners!" Sam chuckled. "My name is Sam."

"Ah! Good to meet you, Sam. Will you be drinking with us tonight then?" he asked the journalist, igniting his sense of adventure all over again.

"Aye! I believe so," Sam affirmed. The operator called out from the railing a level above them. The language was alien to Sam, but he knew his new acquaintance was being summoned.

"I have to go up there quickly," he excused himself. "Talk to you a bit later?"

"Of course," Sam agreed as the blond man made his way to his friend. "Um, I didn't catch your name!" he hollered at the local.

The man with the folded ponytail looked back at Sam and smiled. "Heri. I'm Heri."

It didn't hurt Sam's pocketbook that much to travel to the Hebrides and back for no reason, apparently, because the food and drink offered at Heri's shindig was worth every penny wasted. It had been a long time since he'd hung out with such a rowdy bunch of fishermen and sailors, but what struck him as most interesting was the storytelling. From what he gathered, these people had a get-together at a different house every week. There they'd sing together about the ancient warriors who'd defended their home, eat and laugh together, and share the latest news about their lives.

Sam, as the outsider, was also afforded a few tales to tell and he elected to share some horror stories about his narrow escapes at the hands of the Order of the Black Sun's secret contemporary existence. What baffled him here was the way in which the Faroese men accepted his remarkable stories without question or contest. He reckoned that the alcohol must have sedated their need for inquisition. Throughout the dirty jokes and hairy tales, Sam became more and more aware that the people here spoke of historical accounts as if they'd just happened yesterday. Not to mention, they spoke as if they'd actually been there.

Soon he discovered that this was why his stories of modern day Nazi organizations didn't even provoke a frown out of them. Everywhere on these islands, even in the atmosphere, there was a timelessness where antique practices prevailed even in the present day and few things assimilated into the modern world. Granted, cities like Tórshavn looked like any other modern city. But as far as the mindset and traditions of the large part of the place were concerned, time had not changed much since before 999 AD. The people of the Faroe Islands had every modern amenity and technological advancement Europe and Scandinavia could offer, but something about them had stayed in the old world of their forefathers – and Sam reveled in that.

"You were taking pictures of where the Brits and Americans had their lookout, right?" one of the men asked Sam.

"Aye, and some other historical landmarks," Sam replied as Heri passed him a shot of Eldvatn, a drink he would regret long after swallowing.

"Now, that *Black Sun* you told us about...did you know that they were up here looking for the Empty Hourglass less than sixty years ago?" the tipsy fisherman asked Sam. "But they couldn't find it, so they took off," he gestured wildly with his free arm, almost knocking a wind chime off its hook outside the porch where they gathered, "all the way down to the Bahamas, then to Greece, the stupid Jerries!"

Some of the men laughed heartily, but a woman among them did not look comfortable with the exposition. Blond and beautiful, she hastened to the peppered fisherman and implored him to be quiet.

"Hello, I'm Sam," the journalist said, smiling at her.

"I know who you are, Sam Cleave. Unlike my father and cousin here, I follow world politics and keep a close watch on foreigners with Nifty 50's waiting on our Grind beaches for a bit of bloody smearing. And I'm not talking about the whale hunting. Go back to Scotland and stop exploiting the hospitality of the locals!" she said, sneering at Sam while Heri and his brother held her back.

"Come on, Johild. Don't be a bitch," her cousin reprimanded. But she jerked her hand free and gave them all a hard look. "If you keep entertaining the vultures, you'll soon end up having your bones picked clean. Are you all blind? They've been doing this to us for centuries and you still permit them our hospitality?" Done for the moment with her tirade, Johild stormed off into the night, heading to her home down the street.

"Just ignore her," Heri told Sam. "Women!"

"Aye," Sam replied in shock, "women!"

"Come, have some more beer," the woman's father chuckled and gave Sam a pat on the back.

"I really can't. You're killing me," Sam objected, but the

people roared in disapproval and slammed another bottle of beer against the Scotsman's belly.

"Drink! Aren't the Scots known for being alcoholically inclined?" Johild's father shouted, evoking a chorus of cheer from the others.

Sam sighed. "Well, can't very well let the side down, can I?" he said to himself before chugging down on the beer. But he couldn't help but feel that the angry woman had had some valid trust issues – issues he wished he could have asked her about. She seemed very upset about what he was doing there and that he was even remotely involved with the thugs of the Black Sun. Maybe that was it. Maybe the reminiscence of her land being occupied in World War II cultivated some sort of hatred toward any outside interference, even the presence of a tourist.

Then again, she'd used photography slang, so Sam decided to look into her reasons, whether she liked it or not.

7

$\mathcal{F}$eeling dreadful after a sleepless night of sobbing about her fate, Nina tried no less than four cups of black coffee before leaving for her ten o'clock lecture. The dark circles under her eyes deceived her faux cheer, but thankfully the morning promised that the day would be a very cold one. It meant that she could wear her thick-knitted beanie without having to explain anything. Feeling miserable both mentally and physically, she dragged her diminishing body over the lawn that led into the botanical beauty of the small courtyard garden where an old, lonely cement fountain stood abandoned.

At night Nina could not help but be freaked out by the stone ornament that resembled a human shape when the light fell just right against it. The curtains on her window facing the garden were always drawn for this very reason. But during the day it was clearly a shapely, hand-sculpted fount. Corrosion and age had chipped away at it, but the trough at its bottom was still leak-free and watertight.

The frigid air was biting at Nina's frail cheeks, coloring her nose with a deep pinkish hue. It ravaged her ears and neck, forcing her to push up her already plump scarf to shield her skin from the cold, since her hair was not providing cover anymore. Hastily she rushed into the lobby and headed straight for the kitchen to get a hot cup of coffee into her body. Oddly, nobody was in yet from the faculty, and neither was the Dean. His office was shut tight, unlike all of the other mornings when the door had been left wide open for the inviting morning light to push through the open curtains and into the hallway.

"Weird," Nina whispered before continuing on to the kitchen, which she found locked. Deeply disappointed, she swung around hoping to find someone with a key or perhaps someone from the cleaning staff who might direct her to another kitchen somewhere in the substantial labyrinth of corridors, if such a thing existed. "Anyone here?" she cried, sniffling from the effects of the cold weather she'd just braved. "Gertrud! Are you in yet?"

Nina's small frame crept along the walls as she peeked into every office and storeroom on the floor, finding all of them vacant or locked. She checked her watch. It was ten minutes to class. Fearing that she'd be late, she left for the lecture hall. Fortunately for Nina, her students, all of seven present, were as indolent as she was and respectfully indifferent to discussing the new material.

"You look pooped, Dr. Gould. If you don't mind me saying," one of her female students remarked. "I know how you feel. Must be the weather, or the hostel cooking."

Some of the group chuckled at the assumption, but others just sank into their desks and stared blankly at her. One of the more outspoken lads in the class said, "Why don't we just download a movie based on the modern history of biological weapons and spare the lovely Dr. Gould from having to waste her breath trying to keep us interested?"

"Hey!" Nina scowled, pointing at the young man. "Are you insinuating that my classes are boring? Because if you are, I will have no qualms about re-evaluating your recent submission." Her left eyebrow lifted inquisitively while she waited for some wise retort, but the loud student seemed too weary and he just smiled.

Nina took a good look at her tiny class and noticed that each of them looked a bit like she felt. Of the five males and two females, three appeared immensely sluggish. Her illness afforded her the excuse of fatigue – and even the cold weather could bear some blame for the sloth of the students – but she could not fathom the profuse lack of energy between the whole bunch of them.

"Listen, guys, off the record," she said sincerely, "are you just lazy from the low temps and baby-making weather? Or do you feel unusually tired? Aside from possible late night excursions and such, I mean."

"I did play GTA until 3 a.m.," one replied, "but it's not like I got up at the crack of dawn."

Another student, one of the three that were noticeably weak, shifted in her chair. "You know, I'm not one to goof off for no good reason, but I almost didn't come into class this morning, Dr. Gould. I mean, you know I love history studies, but if it weren't for the nightmares last night and this morning that chased me outdoors, I'd still be sleeping, I'm sure."

"Nightmares?" the other female student asked her friend. "Me too, chick. Me too. And you wake up more tired."

"Wait a minute," Nina interrupted, folding her arms and tapping her pen, "are both of you staying at the hostel or are you townies?"

"Hostel, but separate rooms," one girl affirmed. The exhausted looking young man in the second row lifted his hand. "Me too. Hostel. All three of us."

"So you all get the same food served every night, right?" Nina pried.

"Same as you, ma'am," the first girl answered. "Although, respectfully, it doesn't look like you like the food here very much."

"Rachel!" her friend reprimanded softly, gasping at her audacity.

"Oh, that's alright," Nina smiled. "Truth is, I've been stressed lately, so the appetite, you know..." she clicked her fingers and blew into the air, "...vanished."

The students murmured in agreement and sympathy. Nina shrugged. "It's just weird that you bunch of maniacs are so sluggish this morning."

"Old age," Dr. Christa Smith teased from the doorway, where she'd been eavesdropping. "They're just not teenage material anymore." She smiled, waiting for their obligatory protest. She did not have to wait long. A resounding rebuke of her assessment followed by some snickering filled the classroom.

"Good morning, Dr. Smith," Nina greeted amicably. "Welcome to the mid-morning sloth's meeting."

Christa laughed and entered the lecture hall, carrying a collection of papers under her arm. "Don't fret, Dr. Gould, they just need a jump start. How about giving them a surprise oral exam for grading that counts for the semester?"

Nina thought the suggestion was a bit harsh for an understandably slow start to the week, but Christa looked absolutely serious.

"H-how do you mean?" Nina asked. "I've prepared a tutorial and some assignments, but nothing close to a gradable test that could serve as term papers."

"Of course I'm aware of that, Dr. Gould," Christa replied snidely. "But fear not. I have something quite adequate for the subject and the time frame of your lecture for today. These are exams from a few generations ago that we found in the archives, and what better way to study history than to take exams prepared and used in actual recent history?"

Nina's class stared at her in astonishment, but she needed no prompting to assert her position. "Dr. Smith, could we have a word, please? In private?"

"Whatever for?" Christa asked with a smirk painted on her cemented mask. "As far as I recall, I'm the head of the history division here at St. Vincent's, and if I deem these tests viable to enhance the education of our students, then any visiting lecturer must yield to the decision. I'm sure you understand completely, right Dr. Gould?"

Nina's eyes shot daggers at the intruding, self-proclaimed savant of the institution, but she had no choice. Her contract was month-to-month and she had to complete her curriculum before attaining credit for her involvement, which she needed to strengthen her credibility for other ventures. She gave her students a sympathetic glance, but had to concede. "I'm sure your exams will be a walk in the park for the talent of their capacity," Nina said, challenging the department head while enforcing her faith in her students. "In fact," she said as she took the papers from Christa and handed them out, "I trust that they will *obliterate* anything you throw at them."

"There is only one way to find out," Christa grinned derisively at the desperate attempt for the guest fellow to heave her students from their doubts. "But your faith in your students is valiant in any respect."

Nina checked the clock. It was 10:30am, but her superior had sat down at Nina's desk to preside over her class. She gave Nina an empathetic look and whispered, "Why don't you get some food in, Dr. Gould? God knows you look like you could use it."

With a reluctant look at her class, all drudging through the questions on the examination sheets, Nina took her case and her coat and walked out without a word. Well, the words came after she'd left the chamber and entered the hallway – two words. Choice ones at that.

WHEN NINA CAME OUTSIDE to the undercover cafeteria-come-gathering spot for the limited student body, she chose the first bench nearest to the doors and sat down. Furiously, she mumbled while she rummaged through her bag for a cigarette. Then it occurred to her that she'd chucked them out after the sour revelation she'd suffered with her hair.

"Jesus Christ! It seems I'm not allowed any breaks anymore, am I?" she seethed, slamming her bag on the table in the quiet recreation area. "I may as well shave my bloody head and buy a chest of Dominican cigars and be done with it all."

"You are in luck, my dear."

Nina jumped at the sudden voice, but found the harmless smile of Mrs. Patterson beaming down on her. The old lady held out a pack of Marlboros and offered the blue Bic lighter with her other hand. "Personally I despise smoking, because of, you know, the premature aging, but I can't stand seeing such a lovely child so unhappy." She chuckled as Nina slipped one of the fags between her thin fingers and leaned forward for a light.

After pulling a deep one, Nina's eyes rolled back in her head and her face fell into a picture of peace. She exhaled. "You know, Mrs. Patterson, had you not been so pretty I might just have confused you with Satan."

The elderly woman laughed out loud with Nina and shook her head, "Said every man I have ever been with!"

They shared a good laughing spell once more as Nina rushed the nicotine into her system as quickly as possible to calm her down from the killing rage she felt for Christa Smith. It was evident to Nina that Mrs. Patterson had some hidden agenda behind her support of Nina's deadly habits, but she knew that the old lady would not feel comfortable disclosing it until she thought the historian would need to know.

Still, it was in Nina's nature to be straightforward. She hated playing mind games or taking roundabout trips to the truth. Even knowing how the Dean's mother had left her in concerning circumstances sheltered in words of subliminal warning, she still wished she could just ask what was going on. Propriety stopped her from doing so – for now.

"What are you doing, Mrs. Patterson?" Clara Rutherford exclaimed in awe. She'd just seen the two women sitting outside and came rushing toward Nina. She stopped in her tracks just before reaching the historian, realizing that she could not very well slap the cigarette from her mouth, not without suffering a beating of some measure.

"Um, Dr. Gould, are you sure you should be smoking like that? You know it's very bad for you," she said hastily and tried to look friendly.

"You look like you're about to get caught out for doing some-thing illegal, Clara. Relax," the Dean's mother advised sarcastically.

Nina knew that she was in the middle of some kind of power struggle, but she held her tongue to see what was going on between the two of them.

8

*P*urdue woke from a wonderful, dreamless sleep for the first time in ages. This time he knew he was in his own bed, in his mansion, Wrichtishousis. He'd awoken, however, with a sick feeling curled up in his innards. No doubt it was the recollection of the awful surprise he'd endured at Sinclair two days before. Although he hadn't been seriously injured, apart from a nasty blow to his patella and another pounding to the back of the head, the emotional turmoil of what could have happened had he not realized that he was being played was overwhelming.

As a matter of fact, Purdue felt almost violated, having been probed and deceived by someone who was purposely exploiting him for the benefit of whatever wicked god he was serving. He cringed at the thought of what might have befallen him once the charlatan was done tapping the secrets of his mental reprogramming. Purdue literally shook his head to rid his mind of the possible exits he could have taken from this world.

He'd been awake for over a day, occupied at the police

precinct with Lieutenant Campbell in Dundee until early the previous evening. According to the investigating officer, Purdue had been the target of a hit, but the lieutenant could not confirm this. He'd hinted at it, but assured Purdue it was only the product of experience and logical deduction.

Showering hurt this morning. The warm water agitated the bruises and lacerations he'd incurred during the struggle for the gun. The tall billionaire wet his white hair with shampoo and cried out in pain from the swollen bruise at the base of his scalp. "Oh my God! If he isn't dead yet, I'm going to kill him just for the bloody discomfort!" Purdue shouted in frustration.

In fact, he'd been planning to go and check on the progress of his assailant for his own investigative purposes. "I need Sam. I need Sam to find out who this bastard is and why he wanted to poke inside my head. A case of Scotch to the man who guesses who he works for too!"

"An evil warlord from some grisly German era?" his butler asked nonchalantly as he brought in fresh towels.

"My God, Charles, do you want to give me a heart attack so early in the morning?" Purdue exclaimed.

"Apologies, sir," the refined man replied dryly. "But it is past noon, in case you did not know."

"What?" Purdue whimpered. "Are you serious? What time is it? I left my watch in my bedside drawer."

"It is ten minutes past two, sir. Shall I bring you something to eat? You've slept through four meals. You must be famished," the butler said with a slight lift in his solemn voice.

"Yes, thank you, Charles. But just toast. Toast with salt butter," Purdue requested. "And some Bovril."

"To drink or to spread on the toast, sir?"

Purdue peeked over the screen of the shower, his eyes rolling for the decision. "Um, both." He turned to rinse his hair just as Charles was about to leave, but the butler had to halt when Purdue continued his wish list. "And a mushroom omelet with chopped peppers, please."

The butler sighed and waited for more, but only heard Purdue burp under the clatter of the water. "Very well, sir."

WHEN THE BILLIONAIRE had finally eaten his fill under the watchful and very concerned eye of his cook and house-keeper, he climbed the stairs up to his study to catch up on the business he'd neglected while at the police station.

"Shall I get the car ready, sir?" the butler asked from the bottom landing. "Or will you not be going to Dundee anymore?"

Purdue stopped at the top of the stairs for a moment, looking down at his butler. "Actually, yes. Yes, thank you, Charles. I think I should go and visit my former therapist just to see if there is any more cheer I can provide," Purdue said jokingly. "Did Didi bring my financial month-ends this morning?"

"She did, sir. I told her to leave them on your desk," Charles informed him. "She asked that you sign the documents she's marked and that, if you shan't be back by Thursday, you leave them right where she'd left them for you."

"Marvelous," Purdue smiled, wringing his hands. "That'll be all. Thanks, Charles."

Purdue walked briskly toward the open doors of his study, eager to catch up on important payments and settlements, permits and registration applications for some new patents. He was lenient with his travels and business trips, but never with monetary matters. Purdue liked overseeing payments personally, even though he had Didi working full-time as his personal accountant. She was as meticulous as he, sometimes even strict to a point where he felt as if *she* employed *him*, but he still kept an eye on all movements of his money. Didi had left some documents open on his large rosewood desk, marking the places where his signature and initial were needed with colorful, sticky flags.

"Aw, Didi, you are too creative to be an accountant, my darling," he commented, smirking at the colorful ensemble of markers decorating the normally boring and bland collection of typed and printed papers. One by one he perused the wording to make sure that he knew what he was signing for. On the letters and offers sent from his own office to be checked before being sent out globally, Purdue played editor. Not only was he pedantic about grammar and spelling, but it was also very important to the charismatic explorer and inventor to word his correspondence to reflect his business acumen and his personality.

"Odd...," he muttered as his elongated fingers lifted the last envelope addressed to him.

"What is it, Mr. Purdue?" his housekeeper asked as she passed. "Everything alright?"

He looked up at her with a perplexed expression and lifted

the envelope for her to see at a distance. "Look at this. *Orkney Institute of Science*," he said amusedly. "It's peculiar that I would be receiving a statement from my own clinic in Kirkwall."

"Probably a mistake. Why would you be billed by your own company?" she scoffed with a silly smile.

The housekeeper, Lily, was relatively new in his service, yet Purdue and Lily often spoke about personal matters as if she were a part of his family. In fact, most of his staff was treated very amicably by David Purdue and he was not afraid to ask for their advice on small, apparently trivial matters. Of his other avenues of expertise, though, they were worthless as far as opinions went. Of those subjects they hardly had any comprehension, let alone valuable input.

Purdue shook his head and opened the invoice. Lily remained in the room, dusting absent-mindedly at the wooden orb-shaped bookends on Purdue's bookshelf and waiting for the verdict. But he did not respond. Purdue was so quiet while reading the details of the bill from the clinic that Lily was beginning to worry about him. She refrained from interrupting him for her own curiosity only because of his face. Lines sank into his skin at all the wrong places, leaving Purdue with a countenance of shock and sorrow. Then she watched the concern become desperation until his face had become hard again, displaying a form of determination.

"Lily," Purdue said suddenly, and she jumped to pretend she was busy. "Can you please pack a bag for me? Just some clothing for about...five days away will do. I would do it myself but I...," he choked inadvertently, "...I, uh, have some things to tie up here quickly."

"Of course, Mr. Purdue," she replied in her best profession-alism, but her voice was fraught with sympathy for whatever had just punched him. "How soon will you be leaving?"

Turning red at the lids, his moist, light blue eyes pinned her. In the short while that she'd been working for him, she had never seen Purdue lose color like this. "I will be leaving tonight still."

"Very well, sir," she answered and slowly exited his study, pressed to look back, but refraining. Her large breasts rocked in her jersey as she pulled a light jog on her tiptoes to make a quick break for the garden, where she was dying to share the news of the boss's apparently bad news with her colleagues.

Inside the house, Purdue watched her from the window, but he did not care what she was relaying to the others. He did not care that they would worry and guess as to the news on the account sheet. All he cared about was doing something about the illness of Dr. Nina Gould, a carcinogenic illness turned terminal that had been kept secret from him even while he was paying for the treatment of the very disease.

The staff at his Kirkwall clinic had a third degree coming, and then he had to know everything about Nina's condition before he even thought of contacting her. She was a feisty and independent woman even on a good day, but being contacted by the man she blamed for her malady would send her into either a quiet evacuation or a profuse hatred.

Purdue had not forgotten about his foe in the hospital at Hopkins Memorial in Dundee, but he knew Lieutenant Campbell would notify him as soon as the fake Dr. Helberg woke up. Nina was more important, and her time was running out. So Purdue elected to sort out the well-hidden diagnosis and subsequent therapy of her sickness first.

"I wish he wasn't having so much trouble all the time," Lily told Charles. "He's such a nice bloke and all this bad crap is throwing out his well-being, you know?"

"The best thing is to mind our own business, Lillian," Charles reprimanded her in his stable firmness. "I've been here for years and Mr. Purdue has dealt with some really hair-raising situations and come out of it with tremendous resilience. I suggest you keep to yourself and let the man assert his dominance where need be until he is his old self again."

"Do you have any idea what it could be about?" she persisted.

Charles turned his thin, middle-aged face down to her and said only, "No."

Lily had to abandon her prying at that stage and concentrate on preparing her employer's luggage. For the rest of the afternoon she'd encounter Purdue passing by or see him coming out of the bathroom, but she wisely did not engage him in conversation. Apart from bathroom breaks, he stayed in his study, signing papers and arranging Didi's files for her collection the following day.

When Purdue was done with his administrative duties, he descended the winding stairs to the basement level laboratory, vanishing rapidly under the ground floor concrete and laid stone. He'd made it clear that he wanted to be alone.

Locking the door behind him, Purdue sat down in front of his lab computer. The machine was wired to a network of worldwide scientists, physicians, and medical specialists through a special server that linked up a kind of underground system for professionals, inventors, and researchers of a more clandestine nature.

He did not want the bright white light of the laboratory to give him a hospital vibe, so he kept the emergency lights only. In his smaller, personal laboratory he would make contact with the men and women worldwide who knew all the things his own genius did not have knowledge of. Above him the flickering green eyes of the tall machine blinked zealously to accommodate his curiosity, his need for knowledge about lung cancer.

When he logged into the secure, hacker-protected network he stated what specific information he needed.

I do not have a lot of time. This is not a college assignment, ladies and gentlemen. I do not care about the treatments available for lung cancer, only the cellular workings of the illness and how to, hypothetically, reverse them. It matters not how far-fetched or ludicrous. Based on everything you all know about lung cancer, deliver for me a science-fiction method if you have to. Just tell me how cancer works in terms of compounds and chemistry. Speak my language.

9

*N*ina was watching the secret language of intimidation between Christa's minion and Mrs. Patterson, using the show to keep Clara distracted from how fast she could suck on the fag the Dean's mother had gifted her.

So your hair falls out and you keep aggravating the condition? God, you must be burning brain cells by the second, Nina thought as she watched the two women fight as politely as they could to pull the wool over the visiting historian's eyes. They had no idea that they were failing dreadfully, that her deduction was as sharp as ever. The only thing she couldn't figure out about their match was why she was being fought over. Christa and Clara were hardly acquaintances, let alone friends, so why the hell would they care how much she smoked in the first place?

"It's becoming late, ladies," she finally spoke up, rising from the bench and extinguishing her cigarette. "Time to check on my class."

"But Dr. Smith is with them," Clara said, gawking at her.

"Precisely, sweetheart," Nina replied and blessed Clara's face with the last of her smoke, sending her retreating out of the way where she was trying to block Nina off. The petite brunette gave the old lady a nod and a smile.

"Goodbye, Nina," Mrs. Patterson smiled and waved. "See you later, dear."

What they did not notice was that Nina had no intention of going back to the examination hall. Instead, she wanted to find out what all of the peculiar behavior was about. She reckoned that her distrust of the faculty came from her frail disposition and her own insecurities, but she had to admit that the treatment of her students and the unusual hostility between the women was a point of concern. Something was afoot here at St. Vincent's, and for some reason she was in the middle of it.

"How dare you deliberately hinder the process, Mrs. Patterson?" Clara spewed, almost sounding like her superior witch queen friend in control of Nina's class. "We need Dr. Gould to be here for some time still. Her contract has already been paid six months ahead and she is expected to serve her purpose here for at least this stretch of time. You are impeding her progress as if you have authority here!"

Keeping her voice low profited the failed academic nothing. Since the radiation sickness had almost blinded Nina, it had enhanced her hearing by great measures and she could discern every single word spoken in the hoarse whisper Clara used.

"Now you listen to me, girly," Mrs. Patterson announced as she stood up to reiterate her rank in age above the petty little teacher she had no respect for. "I don't care what you think you're going to get from Dr. Gould. What you're doing to her, and to these students, is unethical and downright illegal. I'm only keeping your hideous practices secret because my son asked me to. Do not provoke my anger, because I know all your bloody little secrets, Clara. Yours and theirs."

Nina's heart was racing at the words of the elderly woman and the way her sweetness turned gravely into power. A deep frown formed on the historian's forehead as she tried to decipher what they were talking about.

"The only reason your presence here is tolerated, Mrs. Patterson, is because Christa respects her husband," Clara threatened. "You know that she'd send you away to a rest home, where you belong, in a blink if it weren't for her love for Daniel. If I were you, I'd refrain from stepping into things you have no business with. Why don't you go stay with another family?"

Mrs. Patterson's blue eyes flashed as she stepped up to the bitchy subordinate of a daughter-in-law. "Now you listen. I have no family. I was a war orphan, growing up in a far more horrible situation than you can ever imagine! Do not think for a minute that your juvenile attacks faze me in the least. And neither do those of that harpy whose teat you're dangling from!"

Mrs. Patterson was so infuriated that her voice quivered and Nina felt the same kind of rage welling towards the gossiping waifs of the institution.

What did she mean by what they are doing to my students? Nina wondered from her hiding place behind the corner. Mrs.

Patterson rushed away in the opposite direction, leaving Clara pallid and relieved that, for now, the fight was over. She retreated into the office of the Department Head, across from Nina's little corner.

"Dr. Gould?" the Dean's voice shredded Nina's thoughts.

"Oh, hello Dean Patterson," Nina smiled sheepishly.

"What are you doing?" he asked mildly.

"H-hi-ding?" Nina replied.

"From what?" he asked, starting to smile at her hilarious honesty.

"Dean, why did you choose *me* for this semester at your college? How did you find me and why did you invite me to teach here?"

"You have a very good reputation, as you know. In fact," he boasted, "you're a bit of a celebrity in the academic world. We thought you would be an invaluable tool for us."

"Oh," Nina shrugged, a bit disappointed with his obvious answer. But then the Dean revealed an interesting tidbit that intrigued her somewhat.

"Besides, I have to credit my wife for your acquisition," he bragged with a gentle hand against Nina's arm. "It was she who suggested you – out of the blue – and I must admit, I couldn't have been more pleased with her choice."

"Um, thank you, Dean," she replied modestly while inside her a little flame was ignited, the same pilot light that usually grew into a furnace during previous chases for relics. Something was cooking in Hook, and it was not Mrs. Patterson's dumplings.

"There you are!" Christa cried from the courtyard she'd entered the building from. "I've been looking all over for you, Dr. Gould. Hello darling!"

Dean Patterson kissed his wife and put his arm around her.

Look at how sickeningly wholesome you look. Such a happy couple, Nina mocked mentally under her calm expression. *It begs the question, why she kept her last name, doesn't it?*

"Here I am," Nina said cordially. "I thought I'd stick around until you were done with your experiment on my class." Her sarcasm was more arousing than she realized, which she instantly noticed by the reaction of the Dean.

"What? What experiment are you doing *now?*" the Dean asked his wife. The way in which he asked the question proved to Nina that his wife performing experiments on students did not seem to be anything new to Dean Patterson. It was an alarming notion to say the least, and Nina vowed to check on her students the moment she was released from the obligatory bullshit conversation they were engaged in.

"Relax," Christa told him. "Dr. Gould's wording is more alarming than need be." She gave Nina a reprimanding glare. "She meant that I popped in this morning to give her students a surprise exam. That's all. Right, Dr. Gould?"

"Correct," Nina replied, electing to keep the pressure on while an important player was present. "Will you be marking the exams or have you brought them for me to mark?"

Christa seemed taken aback, but in front of the Dean she had to keep up the ruse of a pop quiz. "They're on your desk in the basement office. I thought it would be only fair if you marked them, as you're their tutor. After all, with your academic prowess a veering from your curriculum would not be a problem, would it?"

"Of course not. I haven't seen the tests yet, but I doubt the results will be favorable, considering how unusually sluggish the class felt this morning. In fact, all of us eating the hostel food seem to be feeling two hundred years old today. I don't think they were up to such a tough assignment," Nina mentioned innocently. But internally, she was choosing specific phrases and words that she thought psychologically related to what was going on between the Dean and his wife.

The Dean turned his head to face his wife. "That would be a redundant practice, darling. These students can't be tested on subjects Dr. Gould has not yet covered."

"Oh come on, Daniel. I'm just keeping them all on their toes," she responded, casting a look toward Nina to make sure she knew that she was included in that group.

"Even Mrs. Patterson thinks I'm too high strung, apparently." Nina chuckled deliberately.

"My mother? What did she say, Dr. Gould?" the Dean asked.

Nina waved it away with a chuckle. "Oh nothing, really. She is very supportive of me. Lovely lady."

The Dean nodded approvingly. Nina watched the tension grow in Christa's face.

"Very protective, but unfortunately Mrs. Rutherford seems to think the poor old dear is some sort of *burden* around here. Treats her like a child, if you ask me," Nina sighed.

"But nobody asked you," Christa sneered.

"Yet it seems that my presence here is pivotal. However, I seem to be stirring up trouble within the faculty and I don't feel all too needed here anyway," Nina said, still playing the Dean.

"Don't be ridiculous!" he stopped Nina, dropping his arm from Christa to lay his hand on the historian's. "Your expertise and interaction with our students has been nothing short of a godsend, Dr. Gould. Do not let anyone make you feel unwelcome or they will have to deal with me."

The Dean was concerned about the way in which his mother was being treated, but his sober and tranquil manner hid it well. He was thankful to Dr. Gould for pointing it out to him. He was no fool. It was obvious that his wife was trying to shut up the historian and even clearer that the two women did not get along.

"Listen, Dr. Gould, I don't see why you should go through all those exam papers when the subjects were not in your lectures. Let's see those as a practice for mid-terms and nothing more," the Dean released Nina and simultaneously rebuked his wife's efforts at schoolyard tyranny.

"Thank you, sir," Nina smiled sweetly, not even granting Christa a look to acknowledge her presence. "I could do with a bit of a break after all the research I did for today's class...you know, that ended up not being used after all."

"No, I agree," he said. "You take the rest of the day and then you can use that lecture for tomorrow. Will that sit well with you?"

"Aye, that sounds reasonable. I just hope the class is more energetic tomorrow," she remarked. "Good day."

With a general greeting Nina excused herself and left in her wake the flabbergasted Christa Smith and the inquisitive Daniel Patterson. A smile broadened on Nina's mouth with every step she took farther away from them. She could virtually feel Christa's eyes burning into her back. When she had turned the corner at the end of the hallway and skipped down the steps onto the small stone pathway toward her cottage, Nina uttered a little laugh at her small victory. If she was going to be antagonized while teaching at St. Vincent's, she may as well make it worth Christa's while.

Traversing the triangular botanical garden stretch, she once again approached the ancient stone fountain that looked like a human form at night. Only this time Nina decided to stop and study the structure, hoping that a familiarity with it would lessen the grotesque impact of it on her.

Behind her, in the protective shade of the high old trees, another human-looking figure approached.

10

*S*am woke up feeling like a cadaver, post-autopsy. His blurry vision gradually became clearer only to reveal that the walls and ceiling around him were not that of his lodge. In fact, he'd only just realized that he hadn't checked into any lodges when he heard the distant gibber-jabber of the Joensens, the hosts of the party the night before. They were in the kitchen, engaged in loud conversation.

"Oh yah," he groaned softly as he tried to sit up from the couch he was lying on. The windows were wide open, curtains flanking the frame. The sharp cloudy daylight stung his eyes. "For fuck's sake," he whispered, surveying the room through slit lids. Sam's head was pounding, but he got up as quickly as he could. Like a strike of a match the blond woman from the night before appeared in his recollection and Sam remembered what he'd stayed a bit longer for. He had to find out more about her.

"He's up!" Heri shouted to the other men still there. From what Sam had gathered, they'd all just keeled over one by one the night before, just as he had. "How did you sleep, pal? My mother threw a blanket over you, otherwise you would have frozen to death."

"Tell her thanks," Sam grunted, petting his brow with a flattened palm to give it some heat for the pulsing hell in his skull.

"Tell her yourself. Mom, this is Sam Cleave, a journalist from Scotland here..." Heri did not want to open the Grind can again, "...on vacation."

Sam gave him a thankful nod as he put out his hand to the small lady behind Heri. But when she stepped in front of her son, Sam was visibly taken aback by her unnaturally youthful appearance.

"Hello Sam," she smiled in a heavy accent. "My English is not as good as my son's, but welcome to the Faroes and to my home. Please excuse my sons and their friends when they get too crazy. It is a herid...herita...they get it from their forefathers."

"Hereditary, Mama," her son grinned and hugged her. "And Scots are as bad as we are. Most of the northern parts of Sam's country are infested with people who come from the same roots as us anyway."

The approving roar from the other men sounded again. Sam had to laugh. It was as if they roared happily whenever something cool was said about them, even if they should happen to be on the other side of the archipelago, it seemed.

"Nevertheless, behave in front of guests, alright?" she reminded her son. "I am just going to take this basket to Hilde at the shop. Behave!"

With her last command she winked at Sam and exited the room.

"Women," Heri said, just as he always did when he felt awkward at their reprimands or outbursts.

"Aye," Sam smiled, although he was positively itching to ask Heri why they all looked half their ages. Granted, most of the men he'd met looked relatively normal for their age, but a lot of the others just defied the science of aging.

"Heri, you know that journalists are naturally curious about all kinds of things, right?" he eased into the subject.

"Yes, nobody knows that better than us here on the islands. Why?" Heri answered.

"I'M CURIOUS…" Sam winced at the looming conversational embarrassment.

"You're wondering why my mother looks like she could have been a child bride?" the local laughed.

Jesus! Dead-on! Sam thought, and then replied with, "Not a child bride, necessarily…why, do you people do that here?"

Everyone in the kitchen bellowed with laughter, but they refrained from either confirming or denying the question. All they did was stuff a plate of rye bread and omelet in Sam's hands, telling him to sit down and relax.

"Seriously though," Sam said slowly, checking the reaction of his host and his friends to keep tabs on just how inappropriate his prying was. "It's uncanny how young some people here look for their age. Man, just tell me, because if you have a pool around here that keeps you all young I would love to have a dip!"

Heri's friends and brothers just chuckled and spoke in their native tongue, ignoring the honest curiosity of the tourist; everyone, except Heri. He gave Sam a long look of consideration while Sam could see that his wheels were turning.

Aye, you want me to know. You want to tell me. So come on, m'boy, tell Uncle Sam what makes you all look so young. Come on! Sam was thinking as he ate, watching the smart man work his brain to accommodate the curiosity of the foreigner.

Luckily for Sam, the other fishermen exited the back door of the house and stepped into the sharp, white light that had been knackering Sam's senses, exacerbating his hangover. Now that he was alone with his new friend he hoped to find out more about the interesting back stories he had heard about regarding the lost Allied gun pits and radio contact stations.

"Why do you think youth is better, Sam?" Heri asked him. It was a question Sam hadn't been expecting, and certainly not one he had an answer for.

"I didn't say I did. I just thought it wouldn't hurt getting some reversal if I could, you know?" Sam replied, hoping that his loose answer would cover more ground.

"Imagine if people didn't grow old at the rate they were supposed to," Heri said. "Just forget about the perks of an extended life force for a second, and imagine what would happen if we had to find a Fountain of Youth."

Sam nodded as he ate, but when he looked up and met

Heri's eyes, he realized the man expected an actual answer. Now he was forced to confront a usually rhetorical question.

It's too fucking early for anything this deep, Sam thought, still working on countering the alcoholic influence on his thoughts. Yet his host expected an answer. "We'd all be as good looking as you and your mum? We'd get laid a whole lot more for a whole lot longer?"

Heri lifted his hand and sank his shaking head. "Sam, I'm serious. Think about it. If nobody died, or if people lived longer at the current rate of procreation, it would take us less than half a century to be out of food, water, and space. I mean, God, the state of the world right now is catastrophic because there are simply too many humans on this planet for the environment to sustain us all."

"I understand exactly what you're saying," Sam agreed, finally sincere. "But perhaps if science could hone the regenerative factors of youth, don't you think it could aid in the cures of age-specific diseases like Alzheimer's or the likelihood of strokes? Osteoporosis? Arthritic inflammation and stiff joints? Look, I'm not saying that there should be an elixir for staying pretty, Heri. The thought of such a possibility just speaks to the scientific edge in me."

Heri peered at Sam and cleared his throat. "Something you don't know about me, is that I'm a textbook scientist too, Sam. And I have a great affinity for physics. But believe me when I assure you this: such a discovery would rapidly evolve into a greed-driven pursuit for beauty, abused for vanity instead of scientific progress or medical solutions. You know this! I know you do. You've seen how the whaling here got out of hand when ill-researched speculation fueled the self-righteous to attack what they could not explain, or control!"

"Yes, I know," Sam replied as he finished his omelet. "I saw that and I, more than anyone, know that the media is the brain of the ignorant. Lazy minds eat up information presented by the media without ever questioning the parts they omit, the parts that can drastically throw a three-sixty on the truth."

"Exactly. If such a thing existed, why would we ever tell you?" Johild snapped at Sam, jolting his heart to jump at her voice.

The Bitch is back, Sam heard his inner bastard announce, but he did not show it. Much as she was abrasive and unpleasant, Sam couldn't deny her beauty and the fact that he enjoyed looking at her. Heri sighed at her mean opening line, but Sam remained docile. "Good morning."

"Are you still fishing for a story?" she asked sarcastically as she emptied the bag she had with her, unpacking some vegetables and *ræstkjøt,* dried and cured meat Sam would soon become quite addicted to.

"I'm just on vacation, lassie," he elected to rear his head a bit. "The only reason I have my Nifty 50 with me is for hot Scandinavian women and stunning landscapes."

"Which hot women?" she asked while Heri held his tongue to relish the tragic sexual tension between his cousin and the tourist.

"That selkie on Mikladalur has had all my lens time so far," Sam joked harshly.

"A statue," Johild scoffed. "Cold, lifeless women. Is that what appeals to you, Sam Cleave?"

"Aye," he cheered, "and they're still warmer than you are."

Heri choked on his tea, making sure his cousin did not see him shaking with laughter.

"And at least the landscapes here have curves a man's eye can follow for hours," he continued for good measure. He had had it with the pretty woman's rude approach to him for absolutely no reason. "So don't flatter yourself that I'm here to report on the bloody beaches or entertain the assumptions of women who don't know me."

Johild was speechless, which was probably a good thing. Had she uttered what she was thinking, her father would probably have been disappointed. She dropped the rest of the food on the cupboard top and walked into the house.

"You just made an enemy for life there, pal," Heri remarked indifferently, adding hot water to his cup.

"Hope she's patient. There's a bit of a queue," Sam shrugged. "Doing what I do, you learn to burn bridges without much sense of loss. It's a pity, but that's the way it is."

Heri smiled. "You know, Sam, I believe I know now why I relate to you so easily. You're one of very few foreigners I don't think of as an idiotic rambler coming to spew judgment at us. You understand the misunderstood, my friend."

Sam gave it some thought and found that the local's point of view made a lot of sense. "I believe I do, aye."

"You understand the misunderstood, because I suppose we have to admit that you are as misunderstood as we are. Most people think of journalists as vultures of ill fortune, or as attention whores who feed on tragedy," Heri explained. "But you, specifically, are not like that. When people hear that I come from the Faroe Islands they immediately hate me for *killing innocent whales in bloody victory and drunken evil*...but none of that is remotely correct. When people hear you are a journalist, they instantly brand you as a dirty carrier of twisted media bullshit out to make us look bad. In essence, you and I, we're one and the same in such issues."

"Maybe there's no fountain of youth here to keep you good looking, my friend," Sam chuckled, "but there must be a mead horn of wisdom around here."

"Now you're talking," Heri laughed. "But I'll not dismiss the lame references to my looks coming from you. I'll take those compliments too, thank you very much!"

11

Over the rolling ebb and flow of smooth, green grasslands, crowned by low-hanging clouds and dark gray skies, the journalist and the local fish farmer drove. It was late in the morning when they reached the first of the destinations on Sam's itinerary – Akraberg.

"Pillboxes?" Heri asked the visiting journalist.

"Aye," Sam said as they walked up to the former British station bunkers. "That's what they called these bunkers during World War II." He lifted his camera and froze in position before clicking off a few frames. Heri chewed on some of Johild's *ræstur fiskur* while watching Sam move from side to side to cover different angles.

"Can I go inside or is it restricted?" Sam hollered from some obscure corner he was moving in behind. Heri nodded to him that it was okay to go in. Sam took pictures of the interior of the small bunkers and felt his skin crawl with awe. Through the moss-covered, crumbling, cement window, he could see his friend's long blond hair lash in the strong breeze, like a flag from a pole. He was still curious as to the age of the man, although he did notice small creases around Heri's eyes and on his forehead, which meant that he was not a boy anymore.

Inside the discolored and eroded walls Sam could feel a distinct presence. Not a firm believer in ghosts, he shrugged it off, but he could not deny that the age and authenticity of the structures impressed and influenced his demeanor. He could feel the company of the British soldiers in there with him, even with only the moaning gusts calling by the position of the corners and air holes.

Outside the stone and mortar structures were overgrown by weeds and virtually eaten by the foliage that had been hugging its sides for all these years. The sea air filled Sam's nostrils as he crouched down for a good upward angle on the water-stained ceiling of the bunker. He could hear the sound of voices for a moment, an unexpected sound that startled him. Sam retreated against the wall of the pillbox he was in, camera at the ready for anything unusual to make its appearance. Again, he heard the rising and falling of voices in argument, but there was nothing in plain sight in front of him.

Then it dawned on him. The voices came from outside: one male and one female. Carefully Sam peeked around the edge of the window hole.

"Oh, great," he moaned. It was the ever-bitchy Johild accosting her cousin again, probably about Sam's presence there. He hadn't yet had time to investigate her, which frustrated him even more every time she showed up. "May as well take the opportunity," he whispered to himself as he took aim with his long lens.

Sam could not deny the photogenic prowess of the angry beauty and he wished he could only have one normal conversation with her without being hauled over hot coals for being an outsider. After he took enough shots of the two locals he exited the pillbox nonchalantly and strolled towards the two arguing in what seemed completely unintelligible gibberish.

"Hey, can you two fight in English, please?" Sam jested. "I can't eavesdrop like this."

They both stared at Sam with straight faces, not amused. He threw up his open hands in a gesture of surrender. "Alright, so the Scandinavians have a different sense of humor. Noted."

"What are you looking for, Mr. Cleave?" Johild came right out. "Why are you really here? You said you were doing an exposé on the Grind, but then you start lurking around the historical sites, taking account of every single location."

"Johild, control yourself," Heri reprimanded, stepping forward just enough to wedge in between the two.

"No, Heri! I don't trust this guy. Do you know who Sam Cleave is? Do you know what he usually gets involved with?" she fumed. "Espionage, subterfuge during sensitive political events, unearthing all kinds of Nazi catalysts and re-implementing their faculties for modern day warlords to use."

"Wait, wait, wait," Sam shook his head as he stepped closer to her, forcing Heri to hold his breath and protectively put out his hands to both parties. "Where do you get this from, Johild? I'm no Nazi propagator, neither am I some bloody spy or whatever you think you know about me. If you have a problem with me, fine. But if you think I'm going to take your verbal abuse because of some fabricated ideas you have about me, think again!"

"Fabricated? Your own woman lost her life because of your recklessness in busting an arms ring!" she retorted.

"It was her story! I only went with her for..." he stopped, sobered and upset.

"For what? For what, Sam?" she insisted, poking at the tragedy Sam was still haunted by.

Heri looked in Sam's eyes and gently pushed his cousin away from the journalist.

"Protection," Sam admitted. "I didn't want her to investigate on her own, to go to the rendezvous point by herself. What happened was not because of my recklessness. She was about to get her big break."

"Enough," Heri said. "Both of you. Enough. My God, why can't we just talk this out? Play open cards, for fuck's sake. If there is some miscommunication, badly reported reputation, whatever, we are grown people. Put it on the table and get this shit out of the way because it's causing me way too much trouble."

With the commotion the three acquired some unexpected company. Johild's father and two other men came over the mounds surrounding the bunkers. The old man exclaimed, "What the hell is going on here? Good God, we can hear you screaming at each other all the way from Sumba!"

"It's been sorted out, Uncle Gunnar," Heri said, giving a look of warning at Johild. In turn, her light blue eyes pierced

Sam's dark pools where his furnace was still burning with anger.

"Doesn't smell like it's sorted out," the old man remarked as he approached. "What are you doing here, Scotsman?"

"Just taking pictures of historical sites," Sam replied. "Besides, I don't have to report to any of you why I'm taking pictures while I'm on vacation, do I? I'm getting sick of this. Look, I get it that you are paranoid about journalists reporting on the whale issue, but for Christ's sake, I'm taking pictures of British barracks and radio stations that I discovered while I was here. If you have something to hide, don't make it my problem, please. Just leave me the hell alone."

Sam turned and walked in the direction of Heri's 4x4, but old Gunnar was not done with him. "You! Scotsman! Don't think you can just walk away without explaining! We will not let you leave, if you're not careful."

Even Johild did not feel comfortable with that threat. She stood next to her cousin, worried for what her father was up to. "Papa," she said softly, "don't."

"Hold your tongue!" her father snapped at her. "You can rip him from the seams but nobody else can?"

"Can we just sit down and talk this out?" Heri bellowed for all to hear. "Christ! You're all throwing threats around, using accusations to make feeble points. Do you all even know what exactly you are bitching about?"

"I don't trust him because of his affiliations," Johild said. "That's my problem with him."

Sam turned and looked at her. "I'm not associated with

Nazis or their sick propaganda, Johild! Do you want to know why I'm taking pictures of the World War II ruins?" he asked, walking back to her and keeping his body language calm, just in case her family thought that he was being hostile. He stepped through the men to face her. "Because I have a friend who is a historian and she would love some portraits of these Allied stations. I also have another friend who loves to travel and explore, and he has a hard-on for religious relics. That's why I'm taking pictures of your land."

Sam's dark eyebrows pulled apart as his frown disappeared, letting the cool midday light into his deep brown eyes. His long wild hair was black against the pale gray sky behind him, alive with the help of the wind as he lurched over her, waiting for her next attack. But Johild was close enough to see him – *really* see him. She had never been this close to him, where she could smell his cologne. Johild said nothing. Her face fell into a restful acceptance.

Behind them Sam could hear Heri sighing in relief, but for a long while none of them said anything. Uncle Gunnar, however, had more questions for the Scotsman. He was not so easily taken by a handsome pair of eyes or Scottish pheromones.

"Sam Cleave," he said loudly in the hum of the breeze, "how were you involved with the Black Sun? I remember those Kraut swine-fuckers like it was yesterday, and any man close enough to them to have his name mentioned at the same time, needs some investigation, you see? So, since we're all asking straight questions and giving straight answers, how about it?"

"In short, it started when I was asked to cover and record an expedition to Antarctica a few years ago, to find the infamous Ice Station Wolfenstein, mentioned in several historical accounts," Sam briefed the old man out of sheer courtesy. To be associated with the Order of the Black Sun was not something he enjoyed. He wanted to set the record straight, if only to a bunch of farmers and fishermen.

"We were all hired to assist the famous explorer and inventor, David Purdue, in locating the elusive Nazi station that most academics and historians insisted was just a conspiracy theorist's fabrication," he continued. "That was the first time we got involved in the dark side of German history. Although we were almost killed by men affiliated with the arms ring Trish and I exposed, we soon became visible on the radar of the Order of the Black Sun. Regrettably, we've had several run-ins with them while trying to uncover Nazi relics used for nefarious purposes to inflict terror and assert dominance on the current world as we know it."

"So you're not in cahoots with the Black Sun? Not that you would admit it if you were," Gunnar asked.

"Unfortunately I'm very familiar with the organization, sir. But I'm not at all connected to them as an ally," Sam assured him. "Now it's my turn to ask questions."

On looking like Gunnar was about to protest, Heri gave him a chastising, but light-hearted "Tsk, tsk, tsk" and the old man was forced to let his honor swallow his objection promptly. "Alright, Scotsman. What do you want to know?"

"It's simple," Sam shrugged. "Why are you so vehemently opposed to my presence here on these sites – the sites of my ancestors, the Brits? What are you so threatened by? It feels as if I might discover something you're trying to hide."

The foreigner's assumption was categorically accurate to them all, but the others thought it best to let the subject of the interrogator's attention do the honors. After all, as one of the elders of the island of Suðuroy, it was only fitting that he took the stage on explaining what they all knew they were protecting.

"I don't know how to answer that, Scotsman," Gunnar replied. And he was quite sincere. He had no idea how to formulate the truth without spilling the secret they were keeping. To them it had not been a secret, not until someone had come prying in the early fifties. Then again, in 1969 and 1985 more came under the same wicked banner, teaching them that outsiders obsessed with their World War II remnants were pests, carrying a sickness. And all islanders knew that pests had to be exterminated.

12

$\mathcal{N}$ina scrutinized the fountain, sinking to her haunches to read the inscription at the base of the centerpiece. It had been etched roughly into the old stone, but not by any professional scribe or mason. The words appeared to be scribbled by a childlike hand, making it all but illegible. With Nina's deteriorated sight, the legacy of her radiation poisoning, it was virtually impossible to discern. Gently, she placed her fingertips against the letters and attempted to feel their characteristics to hopefully read the words.

"Shit, even if this was Braille, I could still not read it," she mumbled as her fingers found the first four letters. Behind her, the figure drew nearer to watch her guess at the words. "A-O-U..." Nina squinted her eyes to feel and read simultaneously. Her sight favored the shade of the overhead branches and thick leaves that filtered out the pale sunlight that marked a mild day, but even so her focus was too blurry.

"That is a 'Q', my dear, not an 'O'," the familiar voice asserted, frightening the cute historian so that she fell ass-first into a thicket behind her.

"Oh my God! Mrs. Patterson, you have to stop scaring the hell out of me!" she panted, cringing at the wet cold of the loose mud on the seat of her pants that would no doubt provoke questions about her fiber intake.

"I'm so sorry, Dr. Gould," the old woman apologized, trying not to laugh at the historian's expense. "Let me help you out of that muddle."

"Muddle?"

"Mud and puddle. I don't know if there is such a word, but it seems quite appropriate, does it not?" Mrs. Patterson smiled as she pulled Nina up.

"You can't keep startling me like this," Nina gasped. "You'll take years off my life."

"I'm really sorry. Seems I have a soft tread after all. You know, I always wondered if my footsteps would become softer as I aged. Old people wane like spoiled fruit. Our cells diminish so that we become lighter and smaller. My goodness, I wonder how tiny you will be at my age?" she rambled as Nina picked up her coat.

She'd been carrying her coat over her forearm and it had fallen when she did, so she reckoned putting it on would hide the suspicious looking mud stain on her Micala-wide leg pants she'd paid a fortune for. Disgruntled by her ruined clothing, Nina tried to keep the conversation mundane.

"Fancy finding you here at this time of day," she told the Dean's mother.

"I don't only lurk at night, delivering food to esteemed historians, you know," Mrs. Patterson played with a very boastful manner. "Sometimes I emerge in the frail sun to visit gardens too."

Nina laughed awkwardly. "That's not what I meant. I just thought you'd taken a sabbatical from bossy academics for at least the next week."

Mrs. Patterson's brow darkened with the mention of Clara's confrontation earlier. "Can you believe that insolent little cow? I mean, I'm the Dean's mother and she talks to me like that! I tell you, Nina, if I were not such a refined lady I would have walloped the disrespect right off her bloody mouth."

Nina was amused by the elderly lady's pride. Mrs. Patterson's feisty nature reminded her of her own. After locking horns with the unbearable Dr. Christa Smith in front of the Dean today, Nina was delighted to have realized that she had, in fact, not lost the trait she thought she had relinquished when she'd become ill.

"Don't let her get to you, Mrs. Patterson. Some women just have an illusion of who they are because of who they serve. Remember that," Nina told her as they walked through the garden toward the cottages. Nina suddenly noticed a loose stone in the path in front of the old lady, but Mrs. Patterson was already right upon it, too late for Nina to pull her out of the way.

"Ooh, Mrs. Patterson, watch out!" was all Nina could manage.

To her amazement the old woman responded with lightning reflexes, quickly leaping to another stone on the side of the pathway and landing gracefully. "Good grief!" she exclaimed. "I could have broken my neck! Thank you for the warning. I'm going to have to let Humphreys know about that loose pebble and have him fix it before one of the students sue St. Vincent's, hey?"

Nina stood still, gaping in astonishment at her.

"What's the matter?" she asked Nina.

Nina was flabbergasted. "How did you do that?"

"Why, I jumped," the amused old woman explained, quite aware that her abilities could stun, but enjoying the admiration nonetheless.

"I know you jumped. I saw that," Nina said. "But how did you pull off that move?"

Mrs. Patterson smiled. "Och, I've always had great balance and coordination. Up until Daniel was conceived I'd been a national level gymnast. Competed in annual sports meets and even took part in the 1960 Olympics in Rome."

"That's amazing!" Nina raved. "Did you get the gold?"

"Nope. Was in second place until I broke my ankle in my final discipline," Mrs. Patterson lamented.

"That sucks," Nina replied sympathetically. "But to be able to say you were there, that you competed...that in itself is a feat not to be sniffed at."

"Just like a real teacher would say," Mrs. Patterson smiled sweetly at Nina. "I ended up working as an RN for most of my life, having a talent for the medical field that most people marveled at. Do you know how many days I wonder just what would have happened had I not sustained that stupid little injury?" Her face lit up for a moment at the thought of her triumph and then seemed to descend into a sad, bleak reminiscence. "Not a day goes by that I don't wonder what could have been."

"I know the feeling, Mrs. Patterson. But you know, sometimes you think losing what you thought your future was is devastating, until you realize what came in its place is so much more brilliant."

"Spoken, again, like a true teacher," the old woman said, smiling again.

Nina smiled in return, but there was a hint of lost ambition in her face. Afraid that the old lady would inquire about the lost opportunities of Nina's life, she quickly directed the conversation to an unanswered question she had.

"Oh, incidentally, Mrs. Patterson," she said with quick curiosity, "what does that inscription on the fountain say? I got 'A' and ...'Q', you said?"

"Yes, yes, that was a 'Q', my dear. The etching says 'Aqua Vitae' and it was carved into the stone when the fountain was just fashioned," she explained. "I think it has always been here in Hook, even before the town was here. When I moved here with my late husband in 1980, Daniel was only six years old, God bless him. And even then, it was already here."

"So you don't know who wrote that? 'Aqua Vitae' means 'Water of Life,' doesn't it? Unless my Latin is off," Nina said.

"That's correct. Whoever etched those words into the

cement knew the secret of the underground river that ran under this town in the Middle Ages," Mrs. Patterson said.

"The Middle Ages? That far back?" Nina asked.

Mrs. Patterson surveyed their surroundings before replying in a hushed tone, "That far back, my dear."

"How do you know that for sure?" Nina asked as they stepped up on her porch under the gathering clouds.

"There was a historian here, just like you, teaching on invitation – on retainer, about twenty-five years ago," the old lady told Nina, pushing her in through the front door to make sure that she could complete her tale inside Nina's cottage. "His name was Cotswald, I think. But he uncovered the underground river and why the fountain was called the Fountain of Youth, so to speak."

Nina locked the door behind them as Hook grew darker from the coming rain. She put the kettle on and lit a cigarette after she showed her guest to her seat. The Dean's mother continued as if she were relieving herself of a heavy psychological load to the ears of a therapist. Nina could tell that she'd been dying to tell someone about it.

"He'd occupied the same office as you are now, but back then it was a proper office and not an archive room, you see?"

"So, he was also invited? He didn't apply for the position of lecturer?" Nina asked, feeling the nicotine rush through her dying cells and not giving a damn.

"He was," Mrs. Patterson affirmed. "But his contract was cut short, I'm afraid. Naturally, after he discovered that the water in the fountain contained some sort of unexplainable elixir that stumped aging, he made the mistake of trying to claim the property by means of a lawsuit against St. Vincent's. St. Vincent's was then owned by my adoptive father, Professor Gregor Ebner. When my adoptive mother died, he buried himself in his academic career and expanded the programs here to branch out from historical studies to the sciences, giving a lot of students an opportunity to attend the college." Mrs. Patterson smiled. "What a crazy old man! Apart from lacking a moustache, my father looked as scatter-brained and exceptional as Einstein...and he wasn't far from being as smart, either."

NINA SMILED at the joy Mrs. Patterson exuded while reminiscing about her father. She didn't want to pry into the orphan's family heritage or ask too many questions, fearing that she may overstep the line. "He sounds like he was an energetic man. I can see clearly that he raised the likes of you, Mrs. Patterson." She gave the subject some time so as not to seem rude for rushing the old woman to spill the beans on the historian and the water table. Tactfully, she linked the two subjects to urge the story along. "So what did your father do about the lawsuit? I hope he sent the historian packing!"

"Oh yes, I was telling you about that," the elderly guest exclaimed, filling Nina with accomplishment. "He sued my father – some ancestral claim or something. I can't readily remember, but my father won the case and the historian had to go back home with his tail between his legs. Serves him right, too!"

"Good," Nina agreed only to win favor. "What did he reckon? How could he prove that the fountain was that old, then? I mean, if it really dated from the Middle Ages, it should have suffered more ruin than that?"

"No, it was beautifully preserved when my father bought the property," Mrs. Patterson admitted. "You see, the font has not always been the center of a garden. It was, in fact, a well in the basement of a great Norman fortress built only two years after the Conquest by a housecarl named Edwin Something-or-other. So when my father bought this property the previous owner, a local developer and businessman, had already demolished the part of the fortress where the well was and turned it into a lavish courtyard to beautify the building and separate the main halls from the servants' quarters."

"Servants' quarters," Nina repeated. She pointed down with her index finger. "These cottages?"

"Och, yes, but substantially remodeled, of course," she corrected. "Don't worry, my dear. The ghosts of soldiers and servants are long gone. We changed this place so much that no spirit or specter could ever recognize the place, let alone find their way around!"

Nina laughed along with Mrs. Patterson, but felt a bit creeped out nonetheless. "And the inscription has always been there?"

"Well, I suppose whoever changed it from a well into a fountain carved that into the stone sometime between the Middle Ages and the previous owner's reign. Lord knows why you would want to label the thing. Wouldn't one want to keep such a treasure unnamed? It seems people have too much ego to keep secrets anymore."

"Aye," Nina agreed. "But now it's dry anyway, so I guess it doesn't matter anymore."

"That's true," Nina's informative guest attested. "It ran dry only recently. The underground spring dried up not more than five years ago." Mrs. Patterson sighed as Nina extinguished her fag. "These days the old fountain holds nothing but rainwater."

13

*A*fter a night of research, preparing the next day's lecture, and tossing under the ghost-repellant bed lamp, Nina struggled to get out of bed. Her body ached and the agony soon reminded her that she was running out of Neurontin and running too low on her back-up supply of codeine to boot. However, she was determined to make it as far as she could without drugging up and she opted for denial for another day.

Intrigued by what she'd been told about the property the day before, she was adamant to pry into the lawsuit from that Cotswald character, just for interest's sake. Besides, Nina needed a distraction from her mundane teaching life, temporary though it was. Between the pain she was suffering in secret and the cattiness of the female faculty members, she certainly needed something to occupy her mind.

What she did not want to admit was that she was addicted to researching and pursuing relics and solving historical mysteries, and that she could not live without chasing some old, buried secret somewhere. She vehemently opposed the subconscious realization that she had, in fact, gradually evolved into a female version of Dave Purdue. The only way in which Nina would have wanted to be Dave Purdue, was financially, not psychologically.

This time, when she passed the old, eroded fountain, she looked upon it with completely different eyes. When she walked past it, it seemed to call out to her, as if it not only held dirty, stagnant rain water, but that within its core a quiet scream begged for discovery, for release.

She shook her head and made for the main building to get away from the enthralling structure. "God, so this is what it's like inside Purdue's brain?" she muttered like a preoccupied madwoman as she rushed to be on time.

The annoying nasal whine of Clara Rutherford shredded Nina's peace. "Good morning, Dr. Gould. Should we get a temp teacher to take your lecture today? You don't look too well."

"Fuck off, fruit fly," Nina murmured as she took a short left away from the toxic lackey before she would have to punch her in the throat.

"Sorry?" Clara asked, unable to hear Dr.Gould's reply. But when the slight historian did not answer, Clara left it at that with a shrug and a scoff. In the lecture hall, Nina was given the silent treatment by her students.

"Oh, come on," she frowned. "Dean Patterson dismissed the bloody exam anyway, so spare me the martyrdom. You do realize that only the syllabus I present counts, right?"

"But Dr. Smith has tenure, Dr. Gould. Doesn't that mean she

can override your authority?" one of the female students asked.

Nina looked sharply at the girl. "Not if I talk to the Dean about it, sweetheart. He is after all, the one who makes the final decisions at St. Vincent's. Just remember that. So, how did you guys manage that test, by the way?"

They threw back their heads. Some groaned and others looked miserable.

"That bad?" she asked.

Her students nodded. The air conditioner hummed incessantly as Nina tried to teach to what felt like a group of comatose adolescents. Constantly she had to cry out a name or a detail just to keep them focusing. At the end of the class she watched them trudge out of the lecture hall, listless and quiet. It was very unlike them.

These were young people who were passionate about historical studies and had always asked to hear about her confrontations with dangerous archeologists or psycho-bitch Nazi hybrids. They constantly challenged Nina's perceptions on certain political systems and the employment of socialism during those dark, cold years she so loved to flash pictures of on her PowerPoint presentations.

Now they did not object, apart from the occasional grunt. They hardly moved to take down notes. Their laptop desktop lights illuminated their faces in pale blue and soft white death masks without much change in expression, even when they spoke to her. Nina was beginning to become alarmed about their welfare. Above dealing with the horrible signs of her medical regression and the anguish of her condition, she now had to keep sharp to unravel whatever strange phenomenon was manifesting all over the campus.

She sat down after class, exhaling heavily. Nina looked over the printed assignments submitted for review from a deadline she'd given her class a week before.

"I still have to get through all this before I can sleep again," she moaned, thinking about the extra time it took to fact check even the details she thought she was confident about while her brain was on fire and her skin was aching. "I miss Bruich."

Languidly she gathered up the sheets of stapled assignments and logged off from her laptop. The projector was still on, beaming a white Cyclops eye against the barren projector screen after she disable the USB. Nina felt her chest burning, but she tried her best not to start coughing, much as she was pressed to. Her lungs felt impotent when she inhaled, as if they were mere strainers sifting particles from air instead of inflating with it. She tried not to panic as she hastened the packing up process. At least in the basement-makeshift-office she would be able to take care of her coughing fits in private and not have to worry about people asking too many questions about her state of health.

Luckily, the faculty was currently under the impression that Nina simply had an eating disorder, in itself not a trivial malaise. Still, it was far less than to explain having contracted cancer after radiation poisoning from Chernobyl due to running from her *hypno-psychotic* ex-lover.

Feeling the crippling pain blossom reluctantly through her chest and back, Nina rushed to get to the refuge of the basement archive room. Due to the upcoming public holiday, most of the students and lecturers had taken the afternoon off; only a skeleton staff remained on duty until the end of the day. Nina had to pass the Dean's office to reach the top landing of the stairs that led to the basement. But as much as the pain pressed her to get to her sub-level hiding place, the sound coming from behind the locked door of the Dean's office was more intriguing.

She could discern the voice of the Dean arguing with his wife, Dr. Christa Smith. Nina's unnaturally powerful hearing yielded something she knew could not possibly have been a coincidence, given her recent conversation with Mrs. Patterson.

"You cannot, Daniel! This is your family's property, for God's sake!" she seethed.

"I can't give up this opportunity, Christa! We'll be set for life if this sale comes through," he said, trying to reason.

"A Cotswald? Think about that for a minute!" she growled. "The last time your family had to deal with a Cotswald your grandfather almost lost St. Vincent's! Now, after all the hell he went through to get rid of that parasite, not to mention the bad reputation this place got after that lawsuit, you want to just let them have it?"

"I'm not letting them have it, for fuck's sake!" he roared as softly as he could in retort. "I'm selling it – for lots of *money*. You love money, remember, Christa?"

"Don't provoke me," she warned.

"My mother is growing too old to stay with us in the long run. I'm sure you can't wait to get her out of our way. If I sell this property to the Costwalds, we can afford to put her in a high-end retirement home where I will no longer have to worry about my mother's medical needs or her emotional well-being. She will be well taken care of and you will be rid of your horrible, terrible hag of a mother-in-law. Wouldn't that make you happy?" his riposte snapped back.

Nina checked behind her and ahead through the long narrow hallway that was almost completely dark from the rainy weather outside. The high ceiling arched gracefully, reminding her of a cathedral, holding all the secrets of those who'd confessed their sins behind closed doors and hushed torment, just like the tirade she was listening to right now.

The shadowy corridor was thankfully void of human presence. Nina was relishing the information that served to fill out the meager details Mrs. Patterson had furnished her with. Little by little the facts were falling into place, although it was probably not even half the story. Suddenly Nina heard footsteps approaching the door. High heels clapped on the wooden floor, growing louder. The last thing Nina heard as she bolted for the refuge of the dark on the staircase was Christa giving her husband an ultimatum.

"I'm telling you Daniel. If you sell this college, I'm filing for divorce. And all your new income from the sale of this property will be swallowed up in alimony."

"What a bitch," Nina whispered to herself as she watched the tall department head storm down the hall toward Clara's administration office.

The pain was becoming insufferable, but at least the looming coughing fit seemed to have abated with all the excitement of eavesdropping. Nina's boots clanged on the iron steps that became cement and rock stairs halfway between the ground floor and the basement. She threw her bags down quickly and fell to her knees to rummage through her purse for the last sheet of the painkillers she still possessed.

Kind of strange how I never feel drowsy down here, she thought as she gulped down the capsule with the last bit of warmed bottled water she had with her. *Maybe the humming air-con is lulling the kiddos to sleep in my lectures, because it can't be my teaching voice.*

Nina literally felt better when she was in the confined space of the basement's cool tomb, and that was unusual, given her fear of small spaces. It was a comfortable and temperate atmosphere, minus maybe the dust from the stacked paperwork and records. While she caught her breath from the searing agony of her illness, Nina remembered the first time she'd heard something she wasn't supposed to at St. Vincent's: that day in the kitchen when she'd overheard the conversation between Christa and Clara about running records for a male person that Christa did not want to do. Could those records have had something to do with the sale of the college? Perhaps it was why Christa didn't want to run them, so that she could mar the sale of the property. Yet Nina had a feeling that Christa's reasons were not based just in her career or her husband's money, but in something deeper. She would profit so much from the sale. Why on earth would she fight so hard to keep the place? What did it have that other places did not?

"Oh my God!" Nina exclaimed. "She is after the underground river, the fountain!"

"Who is after what?" Gertrud asked from nowhere.

"Gertrud, what did I tell you about just suddenly talking to me?" Nina reprimanded the admin assistant.

"I'm sorry, Dr. Gould," Gertrud apologized again. "I just don't know how else to start talking, especially in a quiet room away from other noises."

"We should put a bell around your bloody neck," Nina said, smiling as she rose and placed her stuff on the desk. "Hey, listen, Gertie," she said in a subdued tone, "do you know anything about the records the Dean was looking for?"

The befuddled assistant rolled her eyes back in thought, mulling it around in her mind for a bit. She seemed to grasp something, but still looked a bit uncertain to the historian.

"I'm not sure about this, but I do know that Dean Patterson has been trying to look up a distant family," she replied, hoping to sound smarter than she felt. Shrugging, Gertrud walked to the iron file cabinet in the corner and pointed. "These are the oldest secrets kept by this college, as far as I know. But I'm not sure if they have anything to do with the Dean or what he's looking for."

"Doesn't matter," Nina said. "It's a start. Thanks Gertie."

"Always happy to help," the assistant said before frowning. "Ugh, they're looking for me topside. Will you excuse me, Dr. Gould?"

"Of course. Go on," Nina grinned, happy to be alone to do her spying.

14

———

"I want to know by the end of this business day," Purdue told Dr. Cait. "But keep it professional."

"Mr. Purdue, I had no idea that you did not know about Dr. Gould's condition," the medical scientist insisted. "Please, you have to believe that I was not deliberately keeping her cancer treatment from you. You were aware of the treatment we gave her, the tests, all that..."

"Yes, but that was for radiation poisoning, not lung cancer," Purdue explained, seated on Dr. Cait's office chair like a king taking charge. He was at the Orkney Institute in Kirkwall, looking for answers from his medical staff as to why he hadn't been told about Nina's illness.

"Mr. Purdue, the radiation she suffered was the catalyst to the contraction of her cancer malady. We assumed you knew that her treatment had been altered accordingly. Nobody here had any idea that you didn't know. Only Evelyn knew that the statements were being sent to Dr. Gould for billing and she told me that this arrangement was at the request of the patient. We truly had no idea that you didn't know. You know it would be absurd of us to deliberately withhold information from our employer!"

"Evelyn...she had a car accident, right?" Purdue asked.

"Yes, sir. She'd been sending the statements to Nina directly, as Nina requested," Dr. Cait reiterated. "None of this was kept from you intentionally. It was just...miscommunication."

Purdue felt sick. Not only did the revelation of Nina's cancer rock him to the core, but the circumstances under which he'd found out made him feel betrayed by the few people he trusted. Yet, the more he considered the various factors involved, the more Dr. Cait's explanation looked legitimate. The billionaire gave a long sigh, looking out the window of the doctor's office at the stunning view of the countryside.

"Just keep your eyes and ears open for me, alright? I can't help but feel this subterfuge was more than coincidental," he told Dr. Cait.

"I shall. But I hope you're wrong, Mr. Purdue. We've been such a good team thus far and I'd rather not think that someone here has been hiding anything."

"So, there's nothing you can do to reverse the effects? No cure for her?" Purdue asked.

The doctor shook his head with a somber look. "Not that we know of, short of reversing time back to before she contracted it."

Purdue's eyes widened, but he said nothing. At once he became completely preoccupied by something, but Dr. Cait knew well enough by now not to ask. The genius inventor always went into a daze of far-out ponderings when an idea came to him. "Thank you, Dr. Cait. I have to go back home to do some experiments."

"Um, alrighty then, Mr. Purdue," Dr. Cait replied. "Please drive carefully. This weather is terrible enough to entail building an Ark."

Purdue chuckled dryly only out of courtesy, but his eyes were somewhere else, as was his mind. Dr. Cait knew that expression all too well. In the past, he'd learned that Dave Purdue got that look just before embarking on expeditions for the sole purpose of chasing relics reputed to be a farce.

As he drove off towards the south, Purdue received a phone call. He could hardly hear anything in the pouring rain, but he could tell that it was the Dundee Police precinct.

"Mr. Purdue, could you please drop in to see Lieutenant Campbell at your earliest convenience?" the officer on the phone asked. "The man who attacked you at Sinclair Medical Facility has died from his injuries and there are some details we need you to fill in for us."

"Oh great," Purdue moaned.

"Sir?" the officer asked.

"Nothing. Can't this wait?" he asked.

"I'm afraid not, sir. Lieutenant Campbell has questions only you can help with and it's imperative that he speak to you as soon as possible."

"Alright. I'm on my way," Purdue agreed reluctantly. He had to get back home. Something Dr. Cait had said had clarified a lot. Apart from the guilt of knowing that the radiation exposure had caused Nina's increased risk for cancer, the doctor's inadvertent advice during his jest held more weight that he could ever know.

"I have to reverse time. I have to un-make the progression of Nina's sickness by reversing time," he kept repeating as he braved the tempestuous mood of the skies in the car he'd rented from the local airport company. Through perilous bends of country road he rushed to get to the airstrip where his private jet awaited him. There were just too many places to be in too short a time; therefore, he'd elected to travel by air to get everything sorted out sooner. Nina's time was running out and Purdue was not going to let her die, especially knowing that he was partly to blame for her contracting the illness.

Now he was frustrated with the added concerns surrounding the police investigation into the incident at Sinclair. All of these other matters felt heavy on Purdue's soul. Even he, the normally fearless and cheery solver of problems, was now faced with things not even he could fix, and that made his heart weak with worry. Secondary to his personality seeing prospective failure as a challenge to excel, Purdue couldn't help but feel like he needed a friend to talk to. Little did he know that a friend had already sent him a message that was slumbering away in his e-mail Inbox.

―――――

BY THE TIME Purdue landed in Dundee he'd already planned his experiments, those solutions he would have to construct to save Nina at all costs. As he quickened his pace on his long slender legs to skip the steps of the police station, Purdue continued filling his head with racing alternatives based on the knowledge imparted by his online contributors. They'd shared extensive knowledge with him about cancer and how it functioned on a base level.

But for now, he had to deal with criminal matters.

"Mr. Purdue!" Lieutenant Campbell exclaimed. "Thank you so much for coming so soon, especially in this horrendous piss-down."

The men exchanged handshakes and Purdue followed the investigator to his office on the second floor from the precinct reception area. "Just to let you know, I'm in quite a hurry. So may I ask that we move this along as quickly as possible?"

"Does your life depend on it?" the police officer asked as they entered his office.

"Not mine. But a friend of mine is in trouble and she needs every second," Purdue shared just enough to provide a reason. "So let's get this sorted out. I hear the charlatan came to his end? How did he die? The gunshot wounds? I suppose I'm up for murder?"

"Culpable homicide, actually. But fear not, I'm trying to prove that your assailant did not die as a result of the gunshot wounds, but that his death resulted from murder while confined in hospital," Lieutenant Campbell explained.

"I have an alibi," was the first thing Purdue unintentionally uttered, evoking a good snicker from the investigator.

"We know, Mr. Purdue," he smiled. "But I've reason to believe that Greg Reusch, your fake therapist, was murdered as part of a cover up for the botched hit on you."

THE FOUNTAIN OF YOUTH

Purdue was intrigued after all. Even though he now had yet another thing to worry about – possibly being indicted – the case presented an interesting chain of events to investigate.

"So am I going to be arraigned soon?" Purdue asked, not to determine how much freedom he had left for himself, but for Nina.

"I've requested that they hold your indictment while I find proof of premeditated murder by someone who posed as a hospital visitor or staff member. If I can't deliver this person, or reasonable doubt, you will unfortunately be tried for the indirect murder of the victim," Lieutenant Campbell explained.

Purdue sighed, shrugging at his unbelievable bad luck of late.

"Why are you on my side in this?" he asked.

"Only because I distrust other people *more* than I distrust you, Mr. Purdue," the officer joked. "Look, I concentrate on the evidence at a scene, and although the struggle and the presence of a murder weapon in your room at Sinclair was a bit difficult to blame on either party, the fact that the security camera had been disabled tells me that you weren't the architect of the fake therapist's attack. Another thing," he cleared his throat to gesture the obviousness of the matter, "the therapist was an *impostor of a dead man*."

"I understand," Purdue said. "Forgive me for saying so, but it doesn't take Sherlock Holmes to figure that out."

"Too right, mate," the officer slapped the desktop in agreement. "It's a very clear-cut case. However, with our lack of a suspect and only circumstantial evidence on record, it is *ironically* the justice system standing in our way here. The law and its rigid rules are always a bitch to bend, even to cold, hard logic."

"Just my luck," Purdue replied. "The victim being charged for protecting himself."

"Not to worry, Mr. Purdue. I have five days to prove that someone entered Hopkins Memorial for the explicit purpose of killing the victim to preserve anonymity," the investigator told Purdue as thunder rumbled over the precinct. The flashing lightning that pulsed on the officer's face gave the trouble Purdue was in an unnecessary nuance of horror.

"Now, as for the folder this bloke had on you," Campbell said. "Can you tell me what it was he was effectively jotting down about you that looks like a long division nightmare? And please, explain it slowly, I've never been good at numbers.

Purdue sniffed and smiled. "Those numbers he recorded were not for mathematical use, Lieutenant. Regrettably, they were numeric codes that the so-called doctor..." Purdue halted to find the right words to explain the ludicrous theory, "...harvested from my brain."

The two men sat staring at one another for several seconds while the storm raged outside the window. Chewing on his tongue before speaking, the lieutenant finally articulated his understanding. "So, he...*downloaded*...information from your brain in the form of number codes?" Then Campbell burst out laughing. "Oh my God, I'm sorry Mr. Purdue. I just sound insane, don't I? But that's what my comprehension told me you conveyed here."

Purdue did not laugh. "You are not insane, sir. That is precisely what I was telling you. The mind, like a computer, functions on codes. We don't know this consciously, but with the right kind of programming the human brain will follow orders to a fault when commanded with certain numerical sequences."

The police officer gawked at Purdue as he continued to clarify. "During my apparent therapy, he removed that information from my mind and jotted down what commands were connected to which code strains. For that I am grateful to him, but those records are the Holy Grail for the Order of the Black Sun and therefore, Lieutenant Campbell, they have to be destroyed."

"Holy Mary," the officer said plainly, his eyes still reading Purdue's to ascertain if the man was bullshitting him. "You're dead serious, aren't you?"

"I am. If you're in possession of those medical reports, you have to make them disappear. If the people who did this to me, the people who killed their own scientist to cover this up, find this information, they can brainwash the entire world and use people like puppets to do their bidding."

"Are you talking mass hypnosis?" Lieutenant Campbell asked in awe.

Purdue's urgent expression convinced Campbell that he was involved in something huge. He leaned forward on his elbows and whispered, "I'm talking about the global domination by the fruit of the Nazi Party without even bothering with World War III."

15

---

*L*ieutenant Campbell's eagerness to investigate the Sinclair Facility was renewed after he'd spoken to the former patient of the institution. He even ignored the destructive and dangerous weather to go and see the security officers again.

When he walked in, he was immediately confronted with standoffish behavior from the young acting administration manager, Melissa Argyle. It was nothing he hadn't expected; in fact, he'd been counting on it.

"Good morning, Miss Argyle," he said as he signed in at the Reception desk.

"Oh, hello Lieutenant," she replied. "I thought you got all you were looking for last time."

"I did from you. Thanks," he answered in his usual condescending way. "But I'm not here to see you, so no need to worry about my taking up too much of your time today."

He expected her to be relieved, but Melissa looked unsettled by his revelation. "Oh? Who, may I ask, are you here to see then?"

"Respectfully, Miss Argyle," he replied, "not you. And that makes my visit none of your business."

Clearly furious, she smiled at him before disappearing behind the partition of the first office. She entered her office and slammed the door. On a hunch, the investigator peeped over the counter at the switchboard at the Reception desk. He smiled when he saw the red light next to her extension light up. She was making a call.

"May I help you, Lieutenant?" the receptionist asked, recognizing him from the last time he was there to investigate the attempted murder of Dave Purdue. Lieutenant Campbell smiled kindly. "Actually yes, you could. May I please see your logbook for the 22nd of January? I need to check all the sign-ins for that day."

Melissa Argyle was on the phone in her office, hoping to get in touch with Guterman, the person she reported to. "The nosy police officer is here again."

While at the Reception area, the investigator was also asking for the phone records of the day, so that he could trace the number Melissa had called after he'd left her office. He had an inkling that the person she'd called after he'd left had promptly orchestrated the assassination of the impostor.

In fact, the investigator deliberately made sure that Melissa saw him there. Applying the heat on her would no doubt prompt her to contact whomever was behind the hit on

Dave Purdue, just as she had the day she learned that this police officer was sharp enough to recognize the sabotage of the CCTV system.

Without fail, the young administrator – who was remarkably unskilled at clandestine practices – played right into the investigator's hands. By using the institution's landline to call her villainous superior in London, she'd left a trail of breadcrumbs in plain sight. Lieutenant Campbell smiled when he saw the pulsing light on the PABX system, delighted that he would soon be able to move in on the perpetrator and spring Dave Purdue from the legal bear trap he'd been caught in.

"Here you go, sir," said the general manager who perused the warrant Campbell handed him. "If you check here," he explained the index of the log book for January, "you'll see that this is the page for all the visitors that day. Dr. Helberg signed in...there, see?"

"Thank you very much. I will have to confiscate this logbook for evidence, as well as the phone records the warrant mentions," Campbell said kindly. "I'll wait. As long as I have that list of numbers when I leave here."

Melissa grew ice cold as she stood, listening to the demands of the police officer. Realizing her mistake, she knew that she too would be killed once Guterman found out that she'd led the police right to him and his organization. Running into her temporary office, she quickly grabbed all of her personal belongings and her raincoat. Flight seemed to be the only way out now. She didn't know what to do, and her heart was pounding under the strain of panic. And rightly so. Guterman, a German national running several assassination cells for the Anglo-Aryan Coalition, was known for his reckless extermination of friends and foes alike. He never needed much encouragement, especially once he felt that someone had screwed up.

"Are you ready to work with us, then?" Campbell asked from behind her. Melissa screamed, her legs buckling under her. The officer scooped her up just as she fell to the ground. Then he laid her shaking body on the couch.

"Oh my God, he's going to kill me! He's going to kill me before the weekend!" she ranted hysterically. "Please, Lieutenant, you have to help me! I needed the money, so I agreed to work for him on the side. He...h-he never said he was going to kill Mr. Purdue. I t-th-thought that Reusch was just supposed to get information during the sessions, I swear!"

Lieutenant Campbell towered over her like a judge, but she'd take that over an executioner any day. His hands rested at his sides. "Relax, Miss Argyle. If you turn state's witness and help us bring in Reusch's killer, you might just survive the wrath of Walter Gateman."

"You know him?" she gasped, as tears came streaming over her cheeks.

"Let's just say, I do my homework," he bragged. "Walter Guterman has been on the Most Wanted list of every anti-criminal website in the known universe since 1968. A war criminal and Nazi ideology propagator, he's pretty notorious amongst black operation commanders."

Campbell sat down next to Melissa. "So, Miss Argyle, how did you get involved with such an unsavory character?"

Suddenly Melissa choked and abruptly ceased her crying. Her wet eyes danced with a miniature madness as she tried to give a normal answer. Slowly she started to shake her head, reaching for a tissue and wiping her nose. Looking world weary, Melissa said, "Lieutenant Campbell, if I told you, you'd never ever believe me."

———

WHILE PURDUE WAS FLYING BACK to Edinburgh with Nina's medical file and payment receipts, his phone rang. The number was prefixed with '298', a number even the world traveling billionaire was not familiar with. Usually he did not feel comfortable answering unknown numbers, especially after learning that he was the target of a hit while admitted at the Sinclair Facility. However, on the other hand, Purdue reckoned that not many people knew his personal phone number, resident on his uniquely produced tablet, so he answered.

He would never admit it out loud, but the sound of Sam Cleave's voice brought him a great amount of joy, cheering him considerably.

"Hey Purdue, how's it hanging over there?" Sam said quickly, but before Purdue could answer he carried on talking. "Have you even checked your e-mail, my friend? I sent you some fantastic pictures from the Faroe Islands last night. Did you get them?"

"Sam! Sam, Sam," Purdue chuckled. "Hose yourself down, lad. I'm on my jet at the moment, so I don't know how badly I want to see bloody beaches and dead whales right now."

"No, that's...no," Sam replied. "That's not all this place is about, Purdue. You have to see the Second World War

THE FOUNTAIN OF YOUTH

monuments and ruins they have up here. It's amazing. Check your mail."

Purdue smiled.

"I shall, Sam. It sounds riveting, really. But I'm a bit tied up in serious matters at the moment," Purdue explained. Still, he decided not to tell Sam about everything that had come to light since they'd last spoken. The journalist sounded way too excited about whatever he'd discovered and Purdue decided to keep the awful truth about their mutual friend, and love interest, to himself until he could tell Sam face to face.

"Oh, alright then," Sam replied, sounding a little disappointed. "Well, let me know what you think when you've had a look. I CC'ed Nina in on the pictures too, by the way, and have heard nothing back from her, either. Is she still in Hampshire doing that teaching gig?"

"I believe so, yes," Purdue answered. His stomach knotted up at the mention of her name.

"Her phone is on voicemail every time I call. I hope the feisty little thing is okay. Sometimes her long silences concern me," Sam admitted.

"I'm sure she is alright. If I speak to her I'll tell her to just drop you a line."

"Probably not my business, Purdue, but you don't sound like yourself today," Sam remarked off hand. Purdue hated keeping the truth from him, even if it were to shield him from a bad emotional crash.

He sighed and let out a small chuckle to set Sam at ease.

"I'm just tired, old cock. Had a rough bunch of days dealing with a lot of crooked people."

Sam paused, leaving the line hanging in dead air limbo before speaking again. "Um, crooked people as in...you know, *those* people?"

Sam's reference to the Black Sun organization was undeniable. Purdue wanted to tell him, but again he elected to let the journalist enjoy his time up beyond the North Sea for now.

"Those people are everywhere, son," Purdue pretended to joke, evading a fib with cleverly fashioned wording. "I've just been inundated with obstacles. Life stuff, you know."

"Aye," Sam replied evenly. Purdue could tell that Sam was withholding.

After another few moments, Sam sighed, "Right. So, uh, get back to me about the photos when you have some off time. Cheerio, my good man."

"Bye Sam. Have a good night," Purdue replied and hung up. He laid back in his comfortable jet plane seat, bringing a glass of Johnny Walker to his lips. There was a long journey ahead of him; not one of flights and driving, but one of experimentation, trial and error, and the immortal chase against the evil arms of the clock. Purdue felt tired already as he wracked his brain for a way to reverse time. It was Nina's only hope and it was his duty as her friend - although their friendship had dwindled severely – and as a scientist – to defy science and employ his great command of physics and technology to save her.

His jet was too close to Edinburgh for him to get any rest, so he surrendered to Sam's imploring and laid his tablet on his lap to check the pictures. If anything, he hoped that some beautiful views and professionally taken images of historical sites would cheer him up a bit.

The screen opened up from the center and flowed outward until the entire image filled it to the extent of the frame of the device. Sam's attachments rung up a total of fifty-two images, but Purdue first read the short message Sam had written in the e-mail body.

Purdue's heart caught in his throat when he read the message, even though he figured it was just his own desperate hope tricking him to make a connection between what he needed and what Sam was reporting. The billionaire sat up as the jet entered Edinburgh air space and glared at Sam's words, reading them a hundred times over to make sure he saw what he thought he saw.

"Holy shit! That's it! Talk about Kismet..." he whispered as he read the words again.

Hɪ Purdue

Here are some awesome pictures from the breathtaking Faroes and a lot of British war remnants I captured as best I could. But I tell you, there are things I can't convey through images. Enjoy!

PS: The women are gorgeous and the firewater is deadly! No wonder I can't get over how these people stay young forever. I swear, time stands still here.

Sam

"A PLACE WHERE TIME STANDS STILL," Purdue gasped. "Quantum physics meets medical application. Of course! How could I not see that?"

As the captain's voice announced that they were about to land, Purdue forgot his fatigue. His heart raced because he could not wait to get started. At last, Purdue smiled.

16

Thus far Sam had only sent Purdue and Nina the images from the ruins at Akraberg, those he snapped before Johild and old Gunnar had showed up with the others. He intended, however, to record all the sites of historical value throughout the islands by the time he was scheduled to return to Scotland. After all, his extended stay merited more footage than just some interviews with locals about the done-to-death whaling debate.

Old Gunnar owed Sam an explanation about his defensiveness towards the journalist. He had to give Sam some clarity on what he was protecting. For Gunnar it was a real problem, because either he had to lie or he had to, God forbid, trust the Scottish tourist. Having already been to Eggjarnar's station, Heri and his family offered to take Sam to the next site while Gunnar told his story.

"There are places here that belong to only us, the descendants of the old Norse people, Scotsman. We just don't like intruders. It's very simple. There's nothing to hide, but some places," he shrugged, "just should be left alone, left to the children of the land."

"I understand," Sam replied, and he wasn't being flippant. He honestly did understand that sometimes you just needed to have your own special place. Sam could see Johild and her cousin exchanging surprised looks.

Even Gunnar had expected more of a fight. Sitting in the back seat next to his daughter, he'd remained quiet since Sam accepted his explanation. Still he could not accede that the journalist was satisfied with just that. The car was abnormally quiet as they drove north inland. Sam, seated in the front next to Heri, spent the next while looking out the window at the wild and ancient beauty of the rocks atop the cliffs wearing hoods of emerald

Suddenly Sam spoke. "Gunnar?"

At once the interior of the vehicle came alive with voices of affirmation. Heri, Johild, and Gunnar mumbled in agreement that they knew there would be more. "Yes?" Gunnar deigned.

"What's this?" Sam asked as he turned in his seat to face the old man seated behind Heri. He passed his cell phone to Gunnar. Upon the large screen of the cell phone there was just one image – a still shot he'd taken from the center of a flattened British World War II ruin at Hvalba during the night, after he'd concluded the day's interviews. Gunnar looked shocked. He pretended to scrutinize the image while he tried to think of a way to dismiss the presence of the peculiar green, blue and pink light particles appearing to hover above the circles of the demolished stone.

Heri tried to peek by craning his neck to use the mirror, but he was unsuccessful. His cousin's wary expression upon seeing the picture concerned him, but he had to watch the road and contain his curiosity until the impending discussion would reveal the subject.

"Where did you take this?" Gunnar asked Sam without looking up.

"Hov," Sam replied without thinking, picking the first town that came to mind.

Gunnar stung Sam with a dirty look. "Don't insult our intelligence, Mr. Cleave. This stone circle is not in Hov. It is at Hvalba."

That was just what Sam wanted to hear. Gunnar realized only afterwards that Sam was testing him, but it was too late to deny its existence. "So you do know about this place? What do you make of the colors hovering over it?"

"I'm not some fancy scientist, Scotsman. How should I know?" Gunnar asked.

"Because you were there before," Sam reminded him. "Move on to the next image on the phone."

Johild took the liberty of helping her father by swiping to the next picture. It was a black and white image, a newspaper cutout from 1969 reporting on a fishing expedition Gunnar and his brother had been on when they'd uncovered the ruin, since then affectionately called the 'Empty Hourglass'.

"What's this?" Johild scowled as she scanned through the article and checked the publication date at the bottom of the article. Astonished, she looked up at her father. He had no words, no explanations. All he did was shake his head, hoping that she'd abandon any enquiry. "What is this, Papa?" Johild insisted with a hoarse panic in her voice. What frightened her, what she was demanding an explanation for was the fact that her father still looked exactly the same.

"What's going on?" Heri asked, not having seen either of the images.

"A photograph from 1969 proves that old Gunnar here has not aged a day since he discovered the Empty Hourglass along with his brother," Sam disclosed. Heri scoffed and snickered at the obvious ridiculousness, but at the looks on his family members' faces he ceased his laughing.

"Wait. Really?" Heri asked Sam, who nodded affirmatively. "How is that possible?"

"Is this what those so-called tourists came after in 1985, Papa?" Johild asked firmly. "Because I remember them asking about the circles when I was twelve years old."

"They were just tourists," he told his daughter.

"Is that why their people killed my uncle in 1969? Because he was a bad tour guide?" she shouted, furious that she'd been deceived all this time.

"Watch your tone, Jo," her father warned, but he knew that she had every right to act this way. Furious at being busted, Gunnar raged at Sam. "Are you happy now, Scotsman? You've been aware of this all this time. Is this why you came here? To break up my family!"

"I'm not the one who lied to my daughter, Gunnar. Your family had nothing to do with my trip here or with the pictures I took. That picture of you and Jon? I discovered it last night while I was doing background research on Johild here," Sam admitted, regardless of the possibility that he could ignite her hate for him again.

"What?" she frowned, now directing her exasperation at Sam.

"I thought you were...*interesting*. I wanted to know more about you." Sam ignored Heri's smirk and retrieved his phone from Johild. At first she was hesitant to return it to him for his insolence, but eventually let him take the phone back.

"Don't worry. There are no pictures of your secrets on my cell," Sam reassured her.

"I know," she snapped. "I have nothing to hide. Not from you," she glared at her father, "or from you."

"Maybe it's better if we go there then, hey Sam? To that circle of stones that I've never heard of either." Heri was hoping his uncle would catch his drift. "It's less than an hour's drive."

Gunnar sank his head.

For many years that made up diminutive lifetimes, he had kept the true reason for his brother's death a secret. He'd bottled up the gruesome incident, not to mention the arcane powers of the two circles that formed the shape of an hourglass, overlapping briefly at a small, singular point from where the alien light source would emerge in exquisite colors.

Johild was in a state of disbelief. She wanted to give Gunnar the silent treatment that worked so well for her mother, but she was not like her mother. She was not as docile as her mother. No, she wanted answers, and she was not afraid to address issues that scratched at her feelings. She looked at Gunnar.

"Papa, I want to know who those people were and why they killed Uncle Jon over a bloody Second World War station!" she said sharply, but without rudeness in her tone.

His weary eyes refused to look at her, but he lowered his voice, recoiling from the fight he'd started earlier in the day. Gunnar was outnumbered by three younger, inquisitive, and fiery personalities and perhaps it was time to come clean to the next generation. It would be better that way. He was tired of remembering and if he told the story he might finally be unburdened from it.

"In 1969 Jon and I went fishing, looking more variety of marine breeding grounds at Hvalba than we could find near our home at Sandvik. I mean, we had children and wives to take care of and wanted to expand our sea haunts," Gunnar told his eager audience. "We took the tunnel that was made that year and packed all the gear we might need for a few days out in the elements. It was summer, so there were no real serious exposure issues to worry about."

"You took a tunnel?" Sam asked. He was thoroughly confused, but Heri explained nonchalantly that there were two tunnels on the island. One reached from Sandvik, which was primarily a coal mining town, to Hvalba.

"Then there was another one built in '62 that leads south toward Trongisvágur from Hvalba. Those are the tunnels my uncle is referring to," he told Sam proudly. The journalist was impressed. "I thought you meant like an underground tunnel or shaft structure," he smiled sheepishly.

"No, pal, those are the two we have. Official tunnels. Nothing as primitive as you're imagining." Heri chuckled as the vehicle sped up under them. He wanted to see the Empty Hourglass for himself, whether old Gunnar's story made sense or not.

Gunnar shifted uncomfortably in his seat and cleared his throat. "Heri, there are actually three tunnels on the islands."

"I don't think so, Uncle!" Heri argued. "I know my homeland better than the rivers that run across it. I've never heard of a third. Sorry."

Calmly Gunnar replied, "Until a moment ago you also did not know about the stone circles either. The people who know about this place you can count on your ten fingers, my boy."

Johild looked at her father. Her face displayed something halfway past anger and heading toward fascination. "How old are you, Papa?"

"I was thirty-nine in that picture," he revealed reluctantly.

The three young people around the troubled old man silently competed to work out his current age first. Heri won.

"Eighty-five?" he gasped. "You mean to tell me my uncle Gunnar is not sixty-three years old, but *eighty...five?*"

"Jesus Christ!" Sam exclaimed involuntarily. "I'm going to have to get a lot more video on you, Gunnar."

"You will do no such thing, Scotsman!" Gunnar roared. "What did I say about exploiting our special places? Our secrets belong to our children. Don't make me drown you in Eldvatn and throw your snooping Scottish ass from a cliff on Hvalbiareidi, because I swear to God I will!"

"Alright, alright!" Sam retreated. "Sorry. Just a reflex. It comes with the job. I'll keep my lens cap on! Relax. You have to understand that this is unbelievable. I thought Heri looked young, but *you*," Sam chuckled in awe, "you take the cake!"

Johild had never been this quiet for this long since her adolescence had hit.

"Can we get back to what happened on Hvalba? I'd like to know before we actually reach the spot. I'd really like to know about the third tunnel that I have no knowledge of too!" Heri pushed his uncle and gestured for Sam to shut up.

"The Scotsman would guess right about the third tunnel, a shaft that ran deep under the mountain. Jon and I, we found it by accident when we needed a rock to hold down our tent that night. We moved the rock and pissed our pants at the glowing ground underneath it," he reminisced humorously, but tears formed in his eyes. "I never imagined that it was the last night I would spend with my brother."

17

Johild's thoughts were racing as she listened to the men talking in the car. Once she'd heard the shocking news that her father had, in fact, been born in 1930, her next question was one for the grand prize. But for now, she waited to hear how her uncle had really died. It might explain her father's hatred of outsiders.

"Jon found the circles first. To this day I'll never understand why nobody ever realized that this mountain was one of the main vantage points from where the Brits dispatched their navy vessels. They used the radio towers similar to the Loran-C's elsewhere in the island." Gunnar frowned.

"So, nobody noticed the circles until 1969?" Heri asked him.

"No. At the time, the land belonged to a British colonel who'd married one of the Egholm girls," he answered, referring to a local girl who'd been in school with them, Elsa Egholm. "The colonel had settled here in Hvalba with his Faroese wife. He tried to make it as a blacksmith or something, as far as I can recall. But then...then *they* came."

Gunnar removed his beanie to wipe the ensuing tears that refused to be denied. For the first time since her previous outburst, Johild felt sorry for her dad. He caught his breath as the vivid memories badgered him. "You know," he sniffed, "the biggest curse of not aging properly is the rampant regrets of bygone times pelting your heart. Make no mistake, I do understand how terrible illnesses like Alzheimer's and dementia must be. But to be young for unnaturally long only means that you have a stronger memory to remind you of a longer timeframe of sorrow. More years of misery...to add to a mind that never forgets."

"Fuckin' hell," Sam said. "That makes so much sense. Really, it makes me think twice about my desire to be young."

"See? What did I tell you?" Heri gloated.

"Aye, you made your point. Gunnar just proved it irrefutable," Sam replied back.

"Uncle, were they the people who killed Uncle Jon?" Heri asked Gunnar.

The old man nodded. "When the Scotsman told of them, when you mentioned those accursed words at the party – *The Order of the Black Sun* – I felt sick. I swore I'd never speak of them again and that if anyone else ever did, I would cut out their tongue."

Sam swallowed hard. "Um, so, tell us what they came here for, Gunnar."

"What do you think they came for, Sam? They were looking for the Fountain of Youth, for immortality. That fucking swine Himmler – it was another one of those twisted projects that he subjected civilians to. You see, when the Brits were stationed on the Faroe Islands during Operation Valentine, some of the soldiers married into the cultures here, just like this colonel who owned the patch of land later. Some of them wrote home about how beautiful it was here and how some parts of the islands have water that preserved the youth of those who drank it," he recounted.

"So this is how you managed to stay young?" Johild finally spoke.

Her father shook his head and corrected her, "Not staying young. We didn't defeat age, my sweetheart. We simply impeded it. How else would I pass for sixty-three when I bathed in the spring at forty years of age? I've aged, but at a delayed rate."

"God, this stuff is riveting!" Sam raved softly. "Absolutely fascinating!"

"And it will stay riveting in secret, right Sam?" Heri put him on the spot.

"Aye," Sam sighed.

"You would make journalistic history if you reported on something equivalent to the existence of God, wouldn't you?" Johild jousted again.

"I would. In fact, it would be the biggest revelation in history. But I'm not stupid enough to share such a thing. Although my closest friends, much like me, would be over-come with awe at knowing that there was a way to deter aging, we are people who know that the human race should not be allowed to harness such a power. Ever. You can rest assured, pretty lassie, that I will never let the sick world out there abuse and exploit something so powerful." Sam hoped that with this speech all of the distrusting ideas in their heads would be put to death once and for all.

"*Pretty lassie,*" Johild whispered condescendingly and rolled her eyes. Sam only smiled.

"As you were, Uncle Gunnar," Heri urged. The vehicle was roaring up the slight slant of the road through the deserted waist of Suðuroy, making good time toward Grímsfjall's hair-raising cliffs.

"Yes, so, the outside world unfortunately learned about the water the British soldiers found to be literally the water of life. Their longevity increased as their health held up. They knew it was no coincidence. As expected of normal, logical people, most Europeans who heard about the miraculous water treated it as a metaphor, you know? They thought it was just a way to say the cleaner air and fresh water was better than the sewers in Europe, right?"

"Yep, I'd have to agree. Something that perfect has to be impossible to most people," Heri remarked as his pristine gray eyes followed the lines of the main road that ran through the island.

"But of course, with the million-and-one level of insanity Himmler and his SS imps possessed, they didn't flinch at the idea at all. Instead, they sent their supernaturally minded ghost hunters to come here and investigate the claims. They sent a team of scientists from the Order of the Black Sun to harvest whatever was in the water the Brits had drilled for up on that mountain back in 1942." Gunnar's eyes held an empty stare while he relived that day. "And they came with a fishing trawler they'd hired, posing as journalists. Who do you think snapped that black and white picture that was used for the article, Sam? It was just our bad luck, me and Jon's, to be there when those parasites showed up."

The old man took a deep breath and carried on, hoping that the trauma would subside a little once he'd passed on the tale. "They asked us about all the British stations, pillboxes, even the monuments like *Minnisvarðin*, for God's sake! Why would they think that magic water would flow out of a stone-carved, commemorative monument?"

"Need I remind you of the ludicrous madness they indulged in, Gunnar?" Sam asked.

Gunnar scoffed and looked amused. "You're right, Scotsman. There was nothing they would not investigate, fucking Kraut demons. I remember Jon being completely engrossed with a woman who was with them, but her husband was with her and they couldn't entertain their attraction."

"Ooh, and was she worth the trouble?" Heri asked, lifting his chin to better see his uncle in the mirror.

"She would've been if she were alone. Beautiful, but sad. You could see by the way her husband treated her that she was probably his victim more than his lover. Poor woman. A Polish national, had a slight limp, but stunning to the eye she was. Her husband, Raymond, turned out to be one of the late Himmler's golden boys, I found out later. You see, my brother and I didn't know at the time that these people had actually been active during the Second World War! They looked our age, but they were a generation above us. Some even older!"

"Wait a minute," Sam stopped him. "Are you telling me that they'd already used this water back in the War?"

Gunnar nodded. "They knew about this life force long before we ever did. I always figured that this was why they didn't think it crazy to look for something like that here too. The Polish woman told Jon that they were on holiday from England, where they lived. She said she'd heard of historical sites where the fountain of youth ran from the stones. Naturally my brother had never heard of anything like that, so we laughed it off."

"That sounds like a mistake," Heri said.

"It was. It was a fatal mistake. After we took them up there they kept us there to *camp* with them, offering to let us use their trawler when we got down to Hvalba. That's when we knew we were in trouble. That was the night Jon and I moved the rock for our tent and saw the glowing ground, but we just replaced it because it frightened us, you know?" Gunnar explained, sounding like a juvenile talking about a prom date. "When the brutes finally went to sleep the pretty woman snuck out to warn us that her organization would never leave us alive, whether they found the fountain or not. You see, their henchmen had unsuccessfully dug all day to find the spring, but the stones of the ruins were bone dry. No spring of life poured from a wet rock or whatever they'd imagined."

"So the spring they were looking for was, in fact, the glowing ground you and your brother found?" Sam asked. Gunnar affirmed with a single nod. "But the Nazi blokes couldn't see it in the daylight, I suppose."

"Plus, it was hidden under a stone, so they wouldn't have

seen it anyway," Johild chipped in. The others agreed with her. "Why didn't you just flee, Papa?"

Gunnar's eyes were heavily laden with emotion. "We tried. Once it was dark we ran away from the camp. But Jon went back to try and save the woman he'd fallen for, to bring her with us." His words broke as his voice failed him. "Hiding a good distance away while I waited for Jon and the girl, I knew something was wrong when she screamed in the quiet tent. I listened to how my brother screamed during the first few blows, cussing and crying out in pain."

The vehicle buzzed as the broken man recalled the moment of his brother's death. There was not a word, nor a whimper, from any of the others listening to his dirge. Gunnar tried to be strong, but his nose was red as his eyes. Sobbing, he finished what he needed to tell them. He made up his mind to tell them everything, and from then on he would never speak a word about it again as long as he lived.

"I ran toward the tent, but it was far and I...I took t-too long to save him. The woman crawled from the tent, her face a bloody mess and through broken teeth sh-she mouthed at me the words... 'he is dead,'" Gunnar forced. His body shook under the strain of his sorrow, but he spoke slowly in order to breathe in between words. "She waved wildly to tell me to run for my life. Th-they...they had beaten my brother to death with a stone...a s-stone...from that very site, and then those godless motherfuckers threw his body over the cliffs where fishermen found his shattered corpse four days later, floating in a churning rock pool at the base of the cliff."

"Christ, Gunnar! I'm so sorry," Sam said softly.

"I'm glad that I told you all the truth after all these years." Gunnar sniffed and wiped his face with his beanie. Johild gave him a few tissues from her bag.

"Now I know why you hate journalists more than I do," she concluded, just as Heri's car slowed down, approaching the last few hundred meters to the rising crest of the very site where Gunnar's tale was set.

18

---

*N*ina was a little concerned about who may be listening, as the small room was missing its door. The narrow stairs ran down from the ground floor and landed right inside the small archive room, leaving no room for a door anyway. She placed her laptop, leather sling bag, and pile of papers on the desk and chair.

Upon her desk the small cooler box stood, stocked with bottled water as she'd requested be delivered every morning. But she had no time for drinks or food, because the incomparable Dr. Gould possessed an innate curiosity that would not be denied. A delicious plethora of information was stacked about her, wall-to-wall records and files others had become too lazy to study. On the other hand, perhaps they put things down here they were afraid might be discovered.

Nina's hunch was riper than she realized.

She vigorously started going through the masses of documents and old files shoved into the cabinet Gertrud suggested might have what she was looking for. Applications, statements of bursaries, and trivial memos about new price hikes and rules of conduct – that was all Nina could find at first. But eventually the large drawers yielded more interesting files, such a lawsuits pending, transfers of property, and letters addressed to prospective benefactors.

"Ewww, if my lungs weren't already full of shit they certainly would be by now. Geez, don't they ever dust down here?" Nina mumbled as her dirty fingertips paged. By now she'd learned not to lick her finger to separate the papers better. The drawers hadn't been touched for what seemed to be decades. Spots and spills on rusted manuscripts tainted the words upon them, but she could discern some of the dates.

"Whoa," Nina whispered to herself, ignoring the steady nausea that came with her slowly creeping chest pain. Her lips moved rapidly as she quickly read short excerpts here and there, but her voice was very subdued and her dusty hands were shaking between the excitement of what she might find and the tremors of her condition. "We herewith wish to welcome you…" she breathed as she took the next document up between her two hands, "…and on retainer, but due to unforeseen circumstances…" She tossed it aside for the next sheet of yellowed parchment, typed out by a typewriter, "…please. Professor Gregor Ebner, Honorary 3rd Level Member and owner of the Norman Fortress now known as St. Vincent's, will be interred this Sunday, 19th of July 1992."

Nina's blood ran cold. Some of the words in this particular newspaper obituary hit home in a very bad way for her. The mention of the term, '3rd Level Member', suggested that

Ebner, Mrs. Patterson's adoptive father, was a member of the Order of the Black Sun. There was no report on how he'd died, however, but it disturbed the pained historian that her good, elderly friend and the Dean's mother, was raised by a member of that sinister organization.

"Oh my God, Mrs. Patterson," Nina moaned as her dark eyes stared up at the ceiling. She had to take a moment to take it all in. Sitting cross-legged on the floor, Nina set that particular snippet aside on the seat of her chair next to her. With the concerning news fresh in her mind she kept on digging into the last drawer right at the bottom of the old locker cabinet.

"More accounts," she sighed, "more kissing ass for money, invitations to awards that don't mean squat, more..." Nina stopped. The next document was far too much of a coincidence for her to dismiss. Her heart went wild as she read it, but to her surprise, her feelings veered towards sadness instead of anger.

"Purdue?" she frowned, keeping the page under direct light from the bulb above her just to make sure she was not reading it wrongly, what with her dwindling eye sight and all. But she would've given anything to rather have had a bout of blindness and been mistaken. Unfortunately for her, she'd read correctly. "Purdue was a benefactor of this college right after the death of Ebner, right as Dean Patterson took over from his grandfather? Holy shit, Dean Patterson is part of the Black Sun! And Purdue is funding him!"

"Dr. Gould?" a voice jolted Nina into a near-heart attack.

"Motherfucker!" she exclaimed, her hand on her chest. With

an extremely apologetic open hand gesture she panted, "I'm so sorry, Clara. Good God, you're worse than Gertrud!"

"What?" Clara frowned, but she smiled at the startled historian who looked so childlike where she sat on the floor. She hadn't make out a word after *'Motherfucker'*, though, since it was the most colorful cry of surprise she'd heard in a long time.

"Nothing," Nina said.

"What are you doing?" Clara asked, amused by the Scottish academic's eccentricity. "Finally somebody decided to clean up down here," she mused as she looked the place over from side to side. "Honestly, Dr. Gould, I don't know how you can work down here. The place used to be a medieval dungeon, for God's sake. Who knows what kind of energy is still down here and you sit here all alone? You have more guts than me.

That's no secret, fruit fly, Nina thought with a mean streak. "Um, can I help you with something down here? I'll be sure to call you if I find a treasure chest of doubloons, okay?" Nina winked.

"Oh! Yes, um, I was just wondering if you will be coming in tomorrow. Dr. Smith just wants to know which faculty members will be using the office building, because they're fixing the air-conditioner or something," she informed the visiting fellow with the high tolerance for creepy atmospheres. Clara shivered visibly, folding her arms tightly across her chest.

"What's the matter?" Nina asked deliberately. It was her own juvenile way of bullying lesser females of the species, especially snobs with no backbone, like Clara Rutherford.

"I don't rightly know, Dr. Gould. But if I can share a secret for a second," she whispered to Nina, "this place has always given me the creeps."

"Aw, this little *tomb*, uh, room?" Nina played.

"The whole college grounds and the main building and even the cottages. You certainly have stones, Nina. But this archive room is far worse than any of the other storage rooms in the rest of this place," she admitted, revealing a side of her Nina hadn't seen before.

She didn't want to admit it to herself, but it appeared that Clara Rutherford was actually just short of pleasant to converse with when she was not around Christa Smith's asshole radar. Nina got to her feet and dusted off her pants. It dawned on her that this was actually the opportune moment to get some information she couldn't get anywhere else.

"Listen, Clara, I've been meaning to ask you," she addressed the obviously uncomfortable woman. "Do you know anyone by the name of Cotswald?"

"Oh, that's the woman that's made an offer to purchase St. Vincent's," Clara revealed, without realizing that she was discussing something Nina was not even supposed to know about. "Why do you ask?"

Nina used a childlike innocence to reel in Clara's knowledge. As long as Nina seemed dumb and harmless, most psychologies dictated that Clara would divulge all kinds of information to her. She shrugged, "Just heard that I was not as special as I thought I was."

"Why?" Clara asked sympathetically.

Nina laughed and waved it off. "No, I just mean that I thought I was the only freelance historian ever invited to lecture here, instead of the usual formal teaching graduates or professors of great universities. I read that a Cotswald person was lecturing here long before me and I got jealous of the tenure he got."

Clara frowned, perplexedly pulling back her head. "No, Dr. Gould. You must be mistaken. He never got tenure."

That's it. Hook, line, and sinker. Keep it coming, fruit fly, keep it coming, Nina coaxed in the shelter of her mind. "Funny. That isn't what I heard."

"No, he was dismissed. Christa and Daniel cut short his contract. They would never nominate him f-f...," Clara suddenly noticed what she was giving away. "Who told you about Cotswald?"

"Mrs. Patterson just mentioned that there was a historian much like me teaching here before. That's all. No big deal. I was just curious," Nina said in the most naïve tone she could manage.

"Mrs. Patterson," Clara sighed. "Of course. Anyway, will you be coming in tomorrow?"

"No," Nina pulled up her nose. "I have a Skype date with a boyfriend and a lot of wine and nicotine on my menu for tomorrow."

"Ah! I see." Clara smiled. "Alright then. I'll let the Dean know."

She started up the stairs again, straining under the mild physical exertion with her plump body before she stopped and bent down to regard Nina through the bars. "Dr. Gould,

I know it's none of my business, but I'd just like to implore you to stop smoking. You know, for your health."

"Oh my darling Clara," Nina replied coldly. "That ship has sailed long ago. Let's just say stopping now would be too little, too late."

Clara did not know how to respond to a statement with such hopelessness from an individual who'd already made up her mind about her fate. "I'm sorry you feel that way, but I guess to each his own, huh?" she replied with a twinge of disappointment. "Those things will be the death of you. I was just trying to help."

"Noted," Nina said, smiling kindly.

She watched the frumpy administration manager's feet slowly take on each step and heard Clara mumbling disgruntledly about Nina's non-compliance and such.

"Looks like you're the one who direly needs a bloody Stair Master," Nina muttered, giving her an eyeful of hate until her feet disappeared from view. "*My* health?" Vexed, she scoffed at the idiot's audacity to chide her on her smoking before sitting down again to find out how Dave Purdue was fitting into a Black Sun member's college funding.

However much she wanted to uncover more on Purdue's involvement, Nina could find nothing more on him in the drawer she was rummaging through. Already annoyed by the nosy administration wench and the growing agony in her chest, Nina felt her anger mounting. One by one she perused the documents she'd found, but the only thing she gained from searching for some proof of Purdue's involvement was a bunch of painful paper cuts and useless letters and staff folders from the eighties, nineties, and early 2001.

"Look at this," she whispered when she discovered the contract of the previous historian, Dittmar Cotswald. "The Dean never invited him here. My God, he was invited to lecture here by Dr. Christa Smith?" Nina looked up. "The same person who invited me here, but why not the Dean himself?"

She nicked her finger again, shortly after sustaining another paper cut mere moments before.

"Shit! Fuck!" she growled. Nina had noticed before that her nose bled a lot more since she'd taken ill, but with her rage and frustration she quickly realized that coughing fits held the same baleful courtesy.

As if Clara's statement had kindled a curse, Nina started coughing profusely. She grabbed a woolen item of clothing she had packed in case of the cold front the weather stations had been predicting and held it in front of her mouth. Nina spewed out globs of blood onto the knitted cardigan as her chest caught fire inside. Her eyes teared up with water as she coughed, her emaciated body convulsing on the floor of the little archive room. On the stairs she swore she could have seen Gertrud watching her, but she did nothing to help. It took little over a minute for Nina to lose consciousness.

19

In the ruckus of the clapping thunder nobody could hear Nina's attack. She was all alone with no way of reaching her cell phone to call for emergency services. The latter did not seem an extreme choice to her by any reach – she thought she was dying. Furious with herself and the world alike, she crawled towards the emergency button in the corner, wired to what she had hoped would be the internal security alarm.

The security panic button, red in color, stood out against the greyish antiquity of the walls that it was mounted on. Nina's weak eyesight could easily identify it, even in the pale light. While clutching her chest and spitting blood into the cardigan, Nina moved gradually over the piles of files and papers she'd been stacking since she'd started her snooping.

Her ears began to hiss and she lost her equilibrium under the force of her body's convulsions just as she reached over the cabinet for the button. On her tiptoes Nina leaned forward to hit the button, but her balance abandoned control and she fell against the cabinet, capsizing the large cabinet with unnatural ease.

In her daze Nina saw the damage her collapse was causing to the wall-lined bookcases and file cabinets, but she was on the verge of oblivion. In her ears the sound of thunder rumbled, but she soon noticed that it was not the voice of the cloudy heavens outside. Toppling the cabinet had caused the wall behind it to collapse just about when she did. By the time Nina hit the ground she knew that the cacophony she heard was her doing.

Knocked out momentarily, Dr. Nina Gould stopped coughing and the cardigan she'd used to shield the bloody mess of her malady fell from her grasp. The rumbling of the crumbling wall eventually ceased, as if it were waiting patiently for Nina to wake up. For a moment she lay motion-less on the floor, never having reached the panic button for help, but her pain revived her. Nina groaned weakly as she tried to prop herself back up to a seated position.

Noticing that nobody has come running to the archive room, Nina was surprised. To her it had sounded like an explosion or an earth-shattering quake.

"How could they not have heard that?" she asked herself as her eyes found the debris of hundreds of years of masonry at the foot of a black chasm in the wall. Blurry sight impaired her scrutiny of what she saw in the large hollowed-out wall, but there was no mistaking what it looked like. Even the blind could see that whatever was in the wall was supposed to remain hidden. What slept inside had been carefully concealed by double walling, as the exte-rior of the two walls was clearly built decades, even centuries, later than the first. Nina squinted her eyes to better discern the details, but soon wished she hadn't.

"Jesus!" she shouted in shock, slapping her hand over her mouth two syllables too late. Her big brown eyes stared, wide, for a moment before she stumbled to her feet and wiped the blood from her nose. It left an ugly smudge of scarlet across her cheek, but she had no time for grooming now. Slowly Nina approached the gaping hole that had split the wall about seven feet from the floor, trying to dismiss the thing she saw inside.

"Oh God, please don't be a corpse. Please don't be a fucking dead body," she murmured as she came closer through the floating curtain of dust. Suddenly she saw it. Gasping, she pinched her eyes shut. "I saw it. I saw it. I saw it and it *is* a fucking dead body..." she whispered in terror, freaked out by her discovery. In her life Nina had seen her fair share of creepy things and even saw people getting killed a few unfortunate times, but to know that she was alone with this corpse in an ancient chamber just exacerbated her repulsion. But much as she felt repulsed, Nina felt a natural compulsion urging her to get closer and investigate her find.

Above her the wild weather exhibited its fury, lending an air of macabre apprehension to the whole affair. "Like being in a goddamned horror flick," Nina muttered, praying that the storm over this part of Hampshire would not knock out the power and leave her in the company of the dead thing under the floor of the main building in the pitch darkness.

Upon reaching the foot of the tear in the masonry the small historian held her breath. In the stuffy ark, reeking of old mud and decay, the figure sat. It had been a full-grown man, from what she could tell by the moldy clothing it was wearing, and it was sitting with its face buried between its knees. Its arms, however, were tied behind its back. The most horrific part of it was that a plate of food had been placed next to a bottle of water – out of reach.

"Christ! How cruel!" Nina exclaimed. Upon closer investigation she noticed that the back of his skull was crushed inside of the skin. It denoted suicide, from the evidence of bone fragments embedded in the wall behind him where his head would have rested. Nina could take no more. Violently she vomited from the grisly and malevolent way in which the man had met his end. "This is sick!" she moaned in between spewing fits. "So fucking sick!"

"You have no idea how sick we can get, Dr. Gould," Dr. Christa Smith said from the staircase. Nina started so that she lost her footing and fell against the ghastly paper-skinned skeleton. She let out a gritty scream, but her true worry was coming down the steps to corral her in. Behind Christa, Clara followed, saying, "I told you she would be snooping, didn't I?"

"Yes, you did, love. Now shut up and let me think," Christa said.

As Clara descended the stairs she pulled down a leather strap, which covered the entrance by trap door.

"And I thought the place had no door," Nina muttered to herself as Christa approached her from the bottom landing. "You could have just denied this, you know," Nina told her, staying in the tight tomb of the ill-fated man to keep distance between her and Christa. Nina saw the gun in Christa's hand and knew that she couldn't escape a bullet with so little space to move in. She knew she was cornered.

"Why would we bother to deny it? They could identify him by dental records and by the timeline of when his wife reported him missing," Christa replied.

"As if she doesn't still hound us to this day," Clara rolled her eyes, getting a deadly look from her friend for it.

"Why don't you shut your mouth and close the trap door, Clara? Make yourself useful!"

"You just love patronizing Clara, don't you? Pity not all people allow you to treat them like shit. Must be hard to find such a loyal door mat," Nina said loudly for Clara to hear.

"Don't attempt to drive a wedge between us, Nina. You'll just embarrass yourself all the more when you know why she is loyal to me," Christa smiled. "You were not supposed to be drained before that fucking nicotine in your blood stream fell considerably, but I guess dirty blood is better than none at all."

"Wow! You're a vampire too?"

Nina felt her feisty nature possess her, just like in the old days when she'd had to take shit from the misogynistic Prof. Matlock at the University every day as fellow in Edinburgh. "No wonder you're such a raging bitch."

Clara and Christa laughed together as Clara pulled a concealed lever that separated the wall opposite that of the tomb where Nina stood. A hidden compartment opened with a deep rumble, the size of a doorway in the rocky wall.

"You don't really believe in vampires, do you, Dr. Gould?" Christa giggled. "Still, you're not very far off in your assumptions."

"Ready!" Clara called from inside the wall. Christa raised the silver barrel. Its Cyclops eye stared Nina straight in the face and she could almost feel the power of the slug splitting her head open. But Christa had far more nefarious ideas. "Move!" she told Nina, cocking the hammer back. With the gun she ushered Nina toward the obscure entrance Clara had opened.

"So, are you going to wall me up as well? What is your problem with historians?" Nina asked sternly, maintaining her condescending sarcasm and hiding that fact that she was terrified.

"Not yet. You see, Dr. Cotswald did not have what you have," Christa said, pushing Nina violently into the doorway.

"If he did, he would have been a girl. Genius!" Nina kept mocking. She imagined all the things Sam Cleave would have spat at his captors. That way she was assured that she would piss Christa off. After all, that was one supremely effective trait of Sam's.

"Don't make me gag you, Dr. Gould," Christa threatened, grinding her perfect teeth. It had always astonished her how cocky her female captives behaved as opposed to the, dare it be said, *stronger* males.

They walked down a small offshoot with a concrete floor that quickly flowed out into an average-sized room, tiled from wall to wall. Even the floor was decked out with white tiling, which was what scared Nina the most.

Killing floor, she thought. *No way they'd tile everything if it didn't get messy in here. My God, I'm a lamb wandering right into the abattoir.* Much as she hated it, it was time for Nina to start playing nice.

THE FOUNTAIN OF YOUTH

"Alright, then tell me and I won't talk back. Why did *you* invite me to teach here? Had it been your husband, I wouldn't have given it another thought. But *you* were the one who got his authorization to send me the offer, Christa. How come?" Nina asked as nicely as she could manage when all she wanted to do was get into a brawl with the self-righteous cow.

Clara wiped the blood smear from Nina's face with a cool cloth.

"Ta," Nina mumbled derisively.

"We need your blood, Dr. Gould," Christa said. Her scowl fell hard on Clara. "Clara, strap her down, for fuck's sake! Are you waiting for her to tip you or something?"

"Why do you let her talk to you like that?" Nina asked, frowning. "Just because she pays your salary, you have to relinquish your self-esteem? Why would you do that for a colleague?"

The two women exchanged glances as Clara strapped Nina to what looked like a dentist's chair, while Christa held the gun uncomfortably close to the historian's face.

"I wouldn't do this for a colleague, Dr. Gould," Clara explained. "I would do it...for a mother."

Nina laughed. "No, seriously. Why would you...?"

She noticed the resemblance between the two women, although one was about a decade the other's senior by the looks of it. Neither of them seemed amused either, which was pretty much their psychology, but there was a disturbing element of honesty in Clara's words and Christa's lack of reaction.

"No. Seriously," Nina forced with a breaking voice, unsure of the unnatural circumstances she was entangled in. Not intending to be cocky this time by sounding like a vain diva, Nina inadvertently uttered, "Jesus, Christa! You look amazing. You *have* to tell me your secret."

Without deeming the compliment worthy of a response, Christa ignored Nina. The historian held her tongue now, imagining the painful way in which she was doomed to die.

Nina's mind raced with thoughts and regrets as her cranium was strapped back onto the headrest of the chair. *Exsanguination? Fuckin' hell! That's a slow and ugly way to go!* Her fear of dying becoming clearer as her chances of escape waned. Nina reconsidered her illness. *I never thought I'd want to live through this cancer shit until now.*

"I don't want to die," Nina said softly, just for good measure, but she knew there would be no clemency from these women. Mute and focused, Christa placed the gun on one of the desks and pulled up her sleeves. "Clara, remove her pants."

20

*H*eri was the last one to step out of the car when they reached the cursed place where, in 1969, his uncles had shared their last night together before one was taken from this earth by the cruel greed of occult-obsessed SS officers. Sam and Johild walked together a few feet behind old Gunnar to allow him some privacy during such an emotional moment. They walked slowly and Heri caught up with them.

"Sam, you're not going to tell anyone about this, right? I'm just making sure, because I don't want my cousin here to tell me she told me so after you betray my trust," he asked Sam sincerely.

"On my mother's life, Heri," was all Sam replied and that was all he had. Fortunately, Heri accepted that out of hand.

"So you're really going to keep all this to yourself?" Johild asked skeptically.

"Aye, but I will show my two friends I told you about," Sam reminded her.

She looked at Heri. "I don't like it."

"Look, Sam, if this gets out, those bastards who murdered my uncle right in front of his brother will return. And who knows which of us will end up being their victims this time, you know? I can't let that happen, as you must understand," Heri told the journalist.

"I understand. Would you feel better about it if I left the cameras in your car?" Sam asked.

The two cousins exchanged glances, considering the offer. Heri moved closer to Sam and gently put his hand on the camera, pressing it downward. "As a matter of fact, that's probably the only way you will leave these islands, my friend."

"Really?" Sam gasped. "You would kill me for this secret?"

"Or keep you here forever," Johild said, only realizing how affectionately promising it sounded after Sam raised an eyebrow and nodded in acceptance.

"Put it away, Sam. You can know the secret, but you can't have evidence," Heri said, making sure the Scotsman heard his ultimatum. "Look at him over there. Look at him."

Sam looked at Gunnar's large frame, wilting and slow in his sorrow where he stood. He was waiting for the young ones, but he didn't turn to see how close they were. He just wanted to stand up there in the icy gusts of Grímsfjall, alone with the spirit of his brother who was thrown from these very cliffs. Gunnar was quiet, but his heart had much to say. When the others joined him he sniffed and said, "There, about fifty meters off, is where we found the Empty Hourglass."

"Is that the name *you* gave it?" Johild asked her father. He nodded and even smiled a little.

"That's what it looked like to us when we stood up on the edge of the cliff and looked down toward it. Little did I know at the time that it didn't resemble an hourglass, yet served a similar purpose. The fact that it was empty was like a poem, you know, a poem about a magical timekeeper without sand. Where time did not pass, no matter on what side of it you were," he mused with a smile. "The glorious glow of the narrow part was really the portal between the time we have and the time we lose, just as it's a passage for the sand to fall through to measure time," he philosophized.

Gunnar took a deep breath, as if he wished to breathe in his brother's ever-present essence. "They left the next afternoon, not having found anything. Those Nazi pigs! When the commando men and the police came up here they played the same game of deceit, saying they were just tourists, journalists who wanted to see the historical sites. By that time my brother was only missing and all I had was my word, see?"

"Aye, they'd have no reason to detain them and the sons of bitches knew it. You didn't come back with the police?" Sam asked.

"No. I was advised to keep away until they had proof that these people were involved, but of course, the rock they had killed Jon with was lying at the bottom of the currents long before the sun even came up that day," Gunnar said as Sam shook his head in disbelief. Gunnar looked him up and down. "Where is your camera, Scotsman?"

Heri stood up proudly. "I forbade him to bring it up here.

Whatever you want to show us tonight, you can show us, but there will be no proof of its existence."

"That takes a lot of pressure off my heart, I must say. Sam, thank you for that," the old man said.

Heri and Johild looked at Sam with reprimanding looks of victory. They had defeated the will of the snooping Scotsman, welcome as he was, for challenging the discretion of the matter.

"You're welcome, Gunnar." Sam smiled and gave the two cousins a mocking look. "I told you that you could trust me."

"Come, I'll show you the place where the two circular ruins meet. But you know, I haven't been here in many, many years. I have no idea if the glowing pool is still here."

"So it's a pool?" Johild asked.

"Yes, the mine shaft the British erected here apparently filled up with underground water from the mountain, forming a subterranean pool. The shaft previously connected the two structures."

"And the colors on Sam's picture?" Heri asked.

"Those were present in the water when I returned a week after my brother was killed. My brother's best friend's father was what would today be called the local police chief. When he went out to question the SS officers, he told them that I'd fallen from the cliff while running away in the night and that my body was found in the bay. Smart man. He knew they'd kill me if they knew I was still alive." He smiled.

"And they bought it," Sam said, smiling. "Lucky for you."

"Imagine how strange it was for me to run into that same

woman in 1985 when she returned with a new pack of dogs? She was older then, but not nearly looking her age. I think she recognized me from back then, but said nothing," Gunnar recalled. "But that time she said she was a dance teacher from England named...um, let me think, she called herself uh, *Cotswald.* Yes! Now I remember. She was Mrs. Cotswald. Maybe she got sick of the Himmler hound beating her up and married a Brit."

"Well, seeing what she was involved in, I would wish that hound had rather beaten her to death, actually," Johild grunted. "She could have helped you and Uncle Jon, Papa."

"But she did," Sam interjected. "She warned them, didn't she? And why wouldn't she acknowledge recognizing your father when she saw him again, if she were so evil?"

"You're protecting a Nazi bitch whose pals killed my family, Sam," she retorted. "Don't protect someone's reputation against my ill wishes until you think about who she really was."

Heri could feel the tension mount between the journalist and his cousin again. Gunnar agreed with Sam to an extent, but he wasn't about to inflame his daughter's wrath again, not here where his brother's memory was sacred.

"So, Uncle, do you think that glowing pool will still be here?" Heri asked out of curiosity and for the sake of peace between Johild and Sam.

Gunnar shrugged positively. "I don't know, but Sam took that picture less than a week ago."

"Remember, that was just a light anomaly above the spot. It wasn't a pool – just a bunch of rocks when I investigated,"

Sam explained about the night he took the picture above the Empty Hourglass.

"It's almost dark," Heri reported, his clear gray eyes surveying the skies and the dying light. "We'll know soon enough."

While they sat vigil at the virtually invisible ruin, waiting for the lights to appear, Sam took advantage of the time to find out a bit more about the anomaly he'd snapped with his Canon a few nights before.

"Heri, I saw your books on science and physics at home. You must have some theory on what this is?" Sam asked.

"Astrophysics is my thing, yes," Heri attested. "But this might be celestial, or at least atmospheric in nature. What would baffle me, though, was if these lights were under the water. So first we have to see if that shaft is still filled with water. If those lights ascend from it, I'll be thoroughly perplexed."

Gunnar laughed. It was a dissociative chuckle that sounded like the mocking of someone who knew when others did not. But he hadn't intended it that way. He was just letting out the juvenile excitement of a boy about to show his friends something awe-inspiring.

"Why can't you young people just enjoy it for what it is?" he asked with a smile. "Why do you have to analyze and study everything to debunk the magic of the beauty we live in?"

Johild smiled, hooking her arm into her father's. "I agree with you, Papa."

"There's no such thing as magic, Uncle Gunnar. We don't take things at face value in the name of God anymore," Heri explained passionately. "The world has evolved into thinking individuals who study and examine things within the scientific spectrum to prove that all things deemed miracles are justified by science. No more do we allow emotion and miracles to steer us and influence our decisions."

"No," Gunnar replied indifferently, "your generation is so engrossed by your scientific theories, to claim knowledge previously privy only to gods, that you neglect to understand that miracles and magic are but the manifestation of wondrous scientific principles. We all know that our world is governed by science, Heri, but to be so rigid in proving magical things a farce is in direct contradiction of living – truly living and enjoying the strangeness, instead of trying to debunk everything that is still wonderful in nature."

Heri sank his head. Of course he disagreed, even just for the use of the words 'miracle' and 'magic.' But he partly fathomed what his uncle meant. He was perceptive enough to see that Gunnar knew the reality of the anomaly, but chose to see its existence as *magical*. The forty-three-year-old nephew of old Gunnar elected to accept his uncle's need to dream and to believe that such things, such as color phenomena under water, were possible.

"Look!" Johild exclaimed. "Is this just psychosomatic of me that I just want to see what my dad is talking about?"

They all got to their feet. Gunnar and Heri looked around them to make sure that there were no other witnesses around them.

"Clear," Heri said.

"As if anybody could come for a walk on a hilltop in this bloody cold!" Sam shivered.

"Scotland is colder, isn't it?" Johild asked mockingly.

Sam leered at her over the collar he'd pulled up to cover his mouth and nose. "Usually, but with the wind chill of your heart, Jo, these islands can grow colder than the Arctic."

"Oh darling, I only make it cold to give you an excuse for the obvious lack of endowment you no doubt sport under those layers of clothing," she hit back.

"Whoa!" Sam gasped, stunned. "That was a really *good* one!"

Heri followed his uncle, who had started toward the higher slope of the mountainside. In passing he sighed at Sam and Johild. "Get a room already, you two. I can smell the sex from a mile away."

21

"Where is it?" Johild asked when she and the other two had caught up with Gunnar. "I saw it a few moments ago. Papa, it looks like the Aurora Borealis, but very small, right?"

He nodded. "That's actually the best way to describe it."

Heri scrutinized the area his cousin had pointed out, but saw nothing. "Are you sure, Jo? I see nothing but flattened stones and long grass."

Sam stood with him, also trying to find what Johild had claimed to observe. Baffled, the four of them stood staring at the site, moving their eyes to widen their peripheral vision, but saw nothing.

"Gunnar, I'm freezing my fucking ass off," Sam said. "Can't we leave a camera here to capture the lights and just stream it to my laptop while we wait in the car?"

"Pussy," Johild mocked, sending her cousin into a fit of

laughter. "Just stick it out, Sam. If it's what I thought I saw, it'll be worth the suffering."

"I'll tell you what. I'll stretch out in the car and you and your toughness can come and summon me when the lights appear, okay?" Sam teased. Heri tapped him on the shoulder and pointed out into the dusky gray of the night, his eyes fixed on something. "What?" Sam asked, but he soon knew what his friend was staring at.

Above the area where the two virtually invisible circles of stone met, a faint play of light shimmered no more than a meter above the grass and weeds that curled under the cold wind.

"Holy shit," Sam gasped softly with widened eyes that were tearing up in the chill of the early night.

Gunnar turned to smile at Sam and Heri, beaming proudly that his word was confirmed. He crossed his arms over his chest and winked. "I told you so."

"Wow," Johild uttered in awe, heading straight for the strange pink, green, and blue haze moving lazily within the confines of some invisible field. "The wind is strong up here. Auroras usually appear stronger with less atmospheric movement, don't they?"

"I suppose," Sam replied. "But I'm no expert on the Northern Lights."

"This can't be the Aurora phenomenon, people," Heri said impatiently, frustrated with their ineptitude at telling basic scientific principles apart. "Those colors in the sky are caused by solar wind in the magnetosphere," he started to explain, sounding a bit patronizing. Gunnar's eyes were stuck on the beauty of the anomaly, while Sam and Jo seemed indifferent to the origin of the phenomenon. It drove him crazy that they weren't concerned with the reason for the appearance of the lights, merely that it was awesome.

"There's no way this occurrence is caused by the same properties of the Aurora Borealis," he said again as they gathered around the floating colors that appeared to intertwine at various points.

"It looks like a paint spill in a glass of water!" Johild observed. The lights illuminated her beauty even more. "Only, there's no ether in which it can blend. Heri, it has to have some sort of magnetic properties," she proposed.

"Jo, the Northern Lights happen at very high altitudes, for one. They don't bob around just off of the ground. And even if they could, they wouldn't just occur within a small area. The atmosphere is consistent throughout the local region on the mound of Grímsfjall," Heri answered.

"Sam?" Gunnar asked. "Why are you so quiet?"

"I'm trying to assimilate both Heri and Johild's theories into my layman's logic to figure out how this is formed, but my conclusions come to nothing," Sam admitted. "You guys will have to let me send this to my friend David Purdue in Edinburgh. He's a genius scientist and I'm sure he'd be able to tell us how it is formed, at least."

"I knew your *sworn to silence* promise was bullshit," Jo grunted.

"It is not. Look, I have no cameras here. What I'm suggesting is getting him over here to see for himself. That way the secret is safe. What do you say?" Sam suggested.

They did not look happy with his offer. "Don't you want to know once and for all what is happening here?" Sam persisted.

"I don't want to know," Gunnar mumbled from the other side of the rainbow shred. "I want this to remain a mystery."

But he was the only one who felt this way. Both the cousins would appreciate some sort of explanation to soothe their curiosity. Sam could see that Gunnar was feeling emotional about having shared his find, so he changed the subject somewhat to draw the old man's attention toward the interesting side of the investigation instead.

"Can we maybe move those rocks away, then?" Sam asked. "Maybe I can just take a water sample if the shaft is still filled with mountain water. That should explain why people who drink it or bathe in it find that their bodies do not age as they should."

Gunnar lifted his chin, looking decidedly more positive about Sam's latest proposition.

"That sounds like a plan, yes," he agreed, and Heri also nodded.

"I have a water bottle in the car," Jo said, and she turned with a skip to make her way down the slope to retrieve a container for their examination. Her long, fair hair looked like a ghostly apparition as Sam watched her disappear into the night.

"Want me to come with you?" Heri called.

They heard her faint voice answer, telling them to get the rocks moved so that they could save some time. They obliged right away under the anxious and excited eye of the old man who had not dipped in the pool since he was a much younger man.

"Watch your feet, Gunnar," Sam said as he and Heri pushed the flat rock aside.

"Geez, are we moving Stonehenge here?" Heri growled as the two of them pushed with all their might, barely inching the stone at all. "This isn't a boulder by any reach. Why the hell is it so heavy? Christ! My rectum is about to prolapse."

Sam burst out laughing and ceased his efforts for a second. "Wait, wait," he chuckled, trying to catch his breath before trying again.

"Uncle Gunnar, how did you and Uncle Jon move this goddamned rock?" Heri moaned as he pushed. His uncle looked a bit confused, having forgotten such small details since that night, but he soon remembered more and more.

"We had our fishing tackle with us, because we were on our way to Hvalba when we ran into the Nazis. That was all we had then that you two don't have now. We also struggled with the stones over that small area, but when I put my pack down on it, Jon could shift it easily," he recounted. With a shrug he gestured that there was no special way he knew of to move the rock. "Maybe you boys just don't have enough marrow in your bones," Gunnar chuckled.

"What was in your fishing bag?" Sam asked him.

"Uh, line, bait, and some iron hooks in my old trunk. We were going to get new nets and rods for different catches once we'd managed to get a trawler at the bay from Ragnar. Other than that, there was nothing worth mentioning."

Sam looked at Heri. "I don't know about you, but it feels like this stone is held by a force other than gravity holding it down. Can you feel that too?"

Heri nodded his head. "What was the trunk made of, Uncle?"

"Copper and tin, mostly. Welded it together ourselves," Gunnar answered.

Sam continued while catching his breath. "As mentioned before, I'm not big on science, but could the copper and the iron in your bag maybe have disrupted an energy field here?"

"Ah! Long shot, but it's the only substantiating explanation," Heri reluctantly agreed. "So there is only one way to find out if it's a possibility. What copper or tin do we have with us?"

Sam shrugged. "None."

Gunnar said nothing. He simply walked over to another, smaller rock and picked it up with a hefty groan. Struggling to get a good grip, he finally lifted the rock high enough to make a good impact before hurling it onto the larger slab of stone. With a crack and a spark, the two ancient stones met, their meeting clap echoing through the vast flatness of the region.

"Fucking hell!" Sam marveled as the large stone shattered from the impact and a faint glow of green light permeated through the crevices of its destruction. Heri stared wide-eyed at his uncle, amazed by the simple solution he hadn't thought of. Gunnar grinned at his nephew, his barrel chest heaving from the exertion. Mockingly he wheezed, "Physics."

Heri had to concede that his uncle had won that bout fair

and square. Sam and Gunnar made quick work of clearing the majority of the stone fragments away to better investigate what was beneath.

"Um, a little help here?" Sam groaned to Heri, who stood sentinel next to him, looking around from side to side.

"Where is Jo?" he asked.

The question sent chills through Gunnar and he jumped up to see if she was nearby, but it had become so dark that the vehicle was obscured by darkness. Sam felt his stomach knot up.

"Johild!" he shouted. "Jo! Where are you?"

"Hey, what are you shouting for?" she said as she came walking from the blackness outside the reach of their flashlights. Relieved, the three men enveloped her to see what container she had brought.

"It's not much," she sighed. "Just 250 ml, but it should be sufficient, right?"

"Aye, that will do," Sam replied, smiling. "Thank you."

Johild was positively spellbound by the beautiful colors floating from the exposed hole. "How did you get the rock away?" she asked, but Heri just cleared his throat. Then she noticed the broken stones surrounding the hole. "It's hard to see if there's water in there behind all this blinding light, but I'll admit, I'm too scared to stick my hand into it."

"We're pretty sure it is made by magnetic particles, Jo," Heri said, setting her at ease. "I'm sure you can touch it." He looked up at Gunnar for support and his uncle reluctantly pretended to be sure.

Johild leaned forward, her hand outstretched towards the ethereal pastels dancing in mid-air. Holding their breath, they waited for a reaction from the anomaly. Looking back at the men, Jo continued on, dipping her fingertips into the colors. The gentle particles merely morphed and mixed until they settled again in a new arrangement. Johild giggled and exclaimed, "It doesn't hurt, but it...it..."

"Tingles," her father said at the same time she did. "Yes, I remember it vividly. The tingling, like when you're walking down a dark corridor and your skin tightens with a thousand little painless needles."

"Adrenaline?" Sam asked.

"Kind of, but there's...more," Gunnar affirmed. "Go on, touch it."

"Will just my hand stay young then?" asked Sam, smiling at the others as he stuck his hand through the dancing haze of green and pink. It was peculiar for sure. He had to lie on his stomach on the edge to get his arm far enough down to reach the water.

"Looks like the water level has sunk a bit," Sam reported, using Jo's bottle to scoop up some water. "I can't wait to hear what Purdue makes of this."

22

"*M*r. Purdue was furious, Charles. He spent how many days in his lab, talking to his science mates on the underground screens and I swear I could hear him crying at some point," Lily whispered to the butler a few doors away from Purdue's bedroom. "It's the first time in over a day that he took to his bed, as you know. So I was wondering if I should even bother with lunch today. Do you think, maybe, what those bad people did to his brain is not gone for good? I mean, his own therapist tried to kill him. I'd be a bit batty if all that had happened to me, you know?"

"Lillian, I told you that Mr. Purdue can get *eccentric* at times, but he is hardly the type who allows his temper, if he had such a thing, to rule him. The man is also well-known as an insomniac, so please stop meddling," the butler advised her.

No sooner did his words sound, than Purdue opened his bedroom door, looking flustered. "Why didn't you wake me at the usual time, Charles?" he snapped as he passed the butler. Before Charles could explain, Purdue slammed the bathroom door and a loud click of the lock confirmed that he wanted to be left alone.

Lily scoffed, looking Charles straight in the eye. "If he had such a thing, hey?"

Gloating at her well-founded concern, she walked down the hallway of the mansion's second story, heading for the kitchen. "I'll slap a nice lunch together then."

"How wonderful for you," Charles sneered to himself. "You guessed right, *once*."

Charles was immensely concerned for his master. He'd never seen Purdue like this before. The jovial billionaire had always seemed to have everything under control. A man who was impossible to offend or intimidate, there had to have been some immeasurable blow to his personal life for his emotions to lurch past cheer, charm, and aptitude. The butler gave it some thought, but he dared not snoop and he would never imagine asking what was wrong. It was simply not his place to do so.

Duty, however, did not deter sensitivity to his master's demeanor. It bothered him that Purdue was behaving completely in opposition to who he really was. When Charles descended the stairs to the laboratories, he once again found the other labs vacant and locked. Purdue had dismissed all the staff members he did not need at the moment and had told them to take a week's paid vacation. Charles knew that this meant that Purdue wanted to be alone.

His laboratory was a mess. Charles was reluctant to clean up, lest he disarrange something he did not recognize as important and that could cost him his appointment as head butler.

"Charles!" Purdue roared from the steamy frame of the bathroom he'd just emerged from.

"Yes, sir?" Charles jogged to get up the stairs to the ground floor lobby.

"Are you in my lab?" Purdue asked, his face contorted in irate seriousness.

"I was just checking if there was any tidying to do, sir," Charles reported, but he could feel his adrenaline warn him that that was the wrong answer.

"Stay out of my laboratory," Purdue barked. "Please! Everyone just stay out of my way. All of you. I'm pressed for time and everything I attempt in my quest to fix this...this... fuck-up..." he shouted, using a phrase that almost never escaped him, "has been a monumental failure. Now, if anyone is looking for me, tell them to sod off. I'm pressed for time." Barely clothed properly, Purdue hastened back down to his lab to continue his relentless search to stop time. Walking briskly as he wiped his face and threw his towel over his shoulders, he mumbled, "No time. Time is running out. Have to stop time, for Nina. Nina, hold on, my dear."

Charles joined Lily at the base of the second staircase from where she'd watched Purdue disappear under the floor. He looked at the cook and admitted, "You're right. The master has gone batty indeed."

The intercom sounded and Charles excused himself to attend to it. In his mind he was already practicing saying '*sod off*' in the most respectful way a butler could. "Yes?" he said into the speaker, with his finger on the talk button. Security reported that a police homicide investigator named Campbell was there to see Purdue.

"Oh drat," Charles mumbled.

"Excuse me, sir?" the man asked.

"Um, nothing, nothing. Let him come in," he ordered. "Thank you."

"Right away, sir."

"Oh, you are just ticking off the boss all over the place today, aren't you?" Lily remarked before she disappeared around the corner to hide in the kitchen.

At first Charles reckoned he could explain the circumstance to the investigator and give his boss what he wished. He opened the front door and changed his mind. The large, rugged man in the typical trench coat worn by noir detectives in old Hollywood flicks did not look like a reasonable man to be told off by a simple butler, that was for certain.

"Good morning. Afternoon. My name is Lieutenant Campbell. I'm from the Dundee office of Police, Scotland," he said in a robust voice.

"Please come in, sir. Mr. Purdue is currently..." he glanced at the direction of the laboratory door, "indisposed for company."

"That's alright, my good man," Lieutenant Campbell consoled strongly. "I'm not here for his company. Where is he?"

"Sir," Charles tried to impede the police officer's way to make him understand reason, but Campbell was not thus inclined. Impatiently, he kept advancing towards Charles as he set out the rules of the way it was going to be.

"Listen, Jeeves. I respectfully urge you to comply with my request or else I will have to arrest you for obstruction and throw you into a cell full of gentlemen you could not groom with a Hazmat suit and a horse brush, savvy?" Campbell hammered his words.

"Very well, sir," Charles replied with a stone face, but inside he wished he had the will and the ability to deck the obnoxious intruder. He kept an eye on the untidy officer as his soles tapped along the descending stairs to Purdue's lab. Taking a deep breath, Charles knocked three times. It wasn't every day he was being shouted at from two sides by two authority figures. Now he just wanted to do his job and go home at 7 p.m. for a hefty brandy and a solid heed to forget the day's bullying.

"What is it?" Purdue's growl emanated through the shield of the door.

"Sir, Lieutenant Campbell is here from the Dundee police offices. He insists on speaking with you, sir," Charles announced as the cop's shadow fell upon him. Alarmed at the prohibited protocol, he was going to ask Campbell to wait upstairs, but Purdue had already opened the door. Charles was caught standing there between the two, awkwardly mute.

"Mr. Purdue," Campbell nodded.

"Lieutenant Campbell," Purdue acknowledged. "You have come far to see me, I presume?"

"Can I see you...in private?" the cop asked, looking hard at the poor butler who was unable to move from between the two men in the confines of the narrow passage.

"Step into my laboratory. We can talk here," Purdue offered and ushered the cop inside. Realizing that the butler would have left them if he hadn't been trapped, a bit of the old Purdue came out as he winked at Charles in amusement and whispered, "You're welcome."

Charles almost smiled as he walked away from the uncomfortable situation.

IN PURDUE'S LAB, Lieutenant Campbell had time to look around as his host tidied up a stray chair for him to sit on. The place was packed with machines, lights, and monitors the likes of which the police officer had only ever seen at MI5 before. The billionaire smelled of fresh Aloe Vera shower gel, but his shirt was clammy from his still moist body and his white hair was unkempt and wet. Even his glasses seemed to sit a little skew on his face and he was barefoot.

"This place...uh," Campbell started. "it looks like you've been busy since we last saw each other."

"Yes, yes, I have. I've been busy with some very important experiments," Purdue said hastily, as he rushed to create some order around the officer. He found two glasses and poured them both some fruit juice he kept in the bar fridge.

"That sounds like Frankenstein stuff. Experiments. Laboratories always gave me the creeps," Campbell admitted as he took the drink from Purdue. "Thanks."

"Oh, don't worry. There's nothing like that going on here.

Just quantum physics and some technological gadgets, but you won't find corpses hooked up to lightning conductors," Purdue soothed him. "That stuff is scheduled for *next* year."

The lieutenant, a sharp judge of character, instantly knew that Purdue was joking. Yet by his background check on the world-renowned explorer and scientist, Campbell knew that Purdue was perfectly capable of such atrocious science.

"I have some new information from a reliable source," Campbell started. Purdue sat down and leaned with his elbows on his thighs to listen as Campbell continued. "Your hit at Sinclair was facilitated by an inside job. Reusch, the impostor, was working under one Walter Guterman, a criminal kingpin we suspect is in alliance with the Order of the Black Sun. It was Guterman who had him killed after he was arrested."

"My God, the Order is like a cancer, tainting cells everywhere," Purdue theorized as his mind's eye ran over the biological crash course in lung cancer he'd been undergoing to help Nina. "And where you cut them out, they just infest another part and grow all over again."

Campbell agreed. "Funny you should say that, Mr. Purdue, because they've spread to another part of your life."

Alarmed, Purdue sat up. "What do you mean?"

"Your holding company, Scorpio Majorus," Campbell read from his notes, "owns the Orkney Institute of Science. Am I correct?"

Purdue nodded, but he felt the pit of his stomach fill with a tempest of bile. He had known something was amiss there, and he was about to find out why.

"My source tells me that someone at your clinic has been leaking information to Guterman, and that this information may have jeopardized the safety of a former patient of your clinic...and a friend," Campbell said. "Dr. Nina Gould."

"Nina? How?" Purdue shrieked.

"Listen, we will locate Dr. Gould and warn her about a possible attempt to abduct her. We have reason to believe that Guterman wants her alive and that he may set a trap via his operatives in England, where she was invited to teach for a few months," Campbell shared.

"Her number is discontinued, at least to me," Purdue lamented, looking dreadfully sad.

"To us as well, but we can locate her from other ways. Don't worry," Campbell said. "Just alert her should she contact you first."

"What does this Guterman want with my clinic? And with Nina? What are we to him?" Purdue inquired.

"Well, I'm not sure how to put this. It sounds quite ridiculous when said out loud," Campbell groaned. "It appears that Guterman and a few other people involved here, are desperately trying to locate..." the cop looked hesitant to say it, "...the Fountain of Youth."

"Excuse me?" Purdue said quickly.

"True story. During the Second World War there was a Nazi project called *Lebensborn* – meaning 'the Fount of Life.' Long story short, there are a few people still pursuing this project and they seem to think Dr. Gould's blood has some sort of resilience," Lieutenant Campbell revealed. "Aside from gathering the information from your mental control, Mr.

Purdue, the bogus therapist was supposed to use you to get to Dr. Gould. Guterman believes, apparently, that Nina Gould holds the Fountain of Youth."

Purdue's face went ashen. "How do you know all this? Who told you?" he shouted in panic. "Who helped them get Reusch in to me?"

Campbell did not have to divulge the information, but he felt that Purdue needed to know.

"Melissa Argyle, aged forty-nine, and a subject of Guterman's *Lebensborn* project since she was nineteen years old in 1966."

Purdue dropped his glass.

23

Three large eyes blinded Nina as Christa switched on the operation lights. The beams were so sharp that even her deteriorated sight was violated. Through her skull behind her eyes the light stung into her brain.

"Did you clean that up?" Christa asked Clara, who nodded.

Nina couldn't see what they were talking about because her head was strapped too tightly to the headrest, impairing her ability to move. From the tray next to her Christa lifted a large, long needle and the fine silver tube flashed with a sheen in the lights above them.

Oh Jesus, no! Nina thought, having great apprehension about the intended entry point of the monstrous instrument. She felt Christa's cold latex touch on her thigh and she tried to kick, but her legs were restrained, both at the knees as well as the ankles, leaving her helpless. Clara had gagged her and waited for Christa's instruction before she'd applied a swab of iodine to the inside of Nina's thigh. Yet, despite all her terror and livid protest, Nina was relieved that the devilish implement was meant to penetrate her skin and tissue alone.

"Sorry if this is a little cold," Clara said as she swabbed the yellow liquid onto a small patch of Nina's skin. She could see in Nina's eyes that what she said was ludicrous to their victim, but she was grateful that she didn't have to hear the verbal abuse Nina would no doubt have flung at her for it.

"This is going to hurt. I'm not going to lie," Christa told Nina as she prepared to sink the needle in. Everyone present knew that the remark was a subliminal mocking towards her nemesis to rub in, if the pun could be excused, the fact that Christa was victorious over Nina.

The historian narrowed her eyes derisively at her tormentor, but it did nothing to avert what Christa was doing. Unceremoniously the department head of the Academy pushed the shaft of the needle into Nina's thigh, slowly plunging it deeper until it had reached the desired depth. Nina's already sensitive skin took the procedure far worse than it normally would have, had it not been inflamed by damaged nerve endings.

With all the breath she had left Nina screamed from the painful stab of the needle, her sick, slight body writhing in agony. Her tears came easily from the anguish of the slow sinking surgical steel that split her skin as it explored her flesh for that important vein. Clara stepped back as if Nina's muffled wails could harm her.

"Get back here, you little coward. Hold down her leg, for Christ's sake!" Christa growled at her daughter. "If she moves too much I could rupture the vein and then she'll bleed out. Is that what you want? Do you want to get old, Clara?"

"No, Christa," Clara replied softly and stepped closer to Nina. She couldn't stand the way in which Dr. Gould's big dark eyes beckoned through pools of tears, but she had to suck it up and deal with it. After all, she was the spawn of an SS officer from Nuremburg, not to mention the other side of her bloodline that was Dr. Christa Smith.

"Now watch closely. This is where we have to keep the femoral artery catheter in place. Are you paying attention?" Christa asked, making sure her assistant was watching. Clara nodded, trying with all her might not to look at the begging eyes of the frail historian and the streaks of tears that wet the temples of her tilted head. All Nina could do to remain calm was to look into the lights, the three huge round suns that would have blinded anyone who had decent eye sight.

With the needle deep enough, Nina's blood began to show in the tubing as the catheter tapped her vein. "Now see, it has to run fast enough to maintain the consistency without bleeding her out too quickly, understand?" Christa lectured while Clara nodded. "Tape down the shaft here, please."

"Isn't she already a bit too pale?" Clara frowned as she caught sight of Nina after securing the draining device.

"Don't fret about that. It's just the shock of what's happening. She'll regain her color for a while and then, when her exsanguination reaches critical level, she will once again get pallid," Christa explained. She looked at Nina with a sickening satisfaction, continuing to jog through the expected regression as if she were sharing it with Nina. "After that she'll lose consciousness and her skin will begin to turn a bluish tint, but don't worry about that. It's just a sign that the oxygen has been depleted."

"Then death," Clara affirmed as her mother removed her surgical gloves.

"Remove the gag. We're not monsters." Christa smiled coldly at her victim as she gave the order to Clara.

Nina would have no reason or benefit in screaming for help. She was very deep and hidden behind enemy lines, probably being left for dead. *Serves me right for cutting ties with Purdue. Serves me right for cutting communication with him and Sam while taking this contract,* she chastised herself. The very same inner voice that had spitefully kept smoking after she'd been diagnosed with lung cancer now punished her for needing to distance herself from Sam and Purdue for a bit to process the illness.

"Why do you want my blood?" Nina muttered wearily.

"Because your blood is special, Dr. Gould," Christa answered. "Since the well dried up here a few years ago we've been looking for something that was as potent as the subterranean water in the cave river under this town."

"Potent? As what?" Nina frowned.

"The Fountain of Youth, my darling. You know that old font in the garden my mother-in-law so readily told you about? That used to be one of the arcane springs on this planet that yielded water that could slow aging – by decades," Christa explained as Clara looked on.

"So...first of all, you believe that this water – which is probably just high in preservative minerals – can make you forever young," Nina asked.

"Take a good look at my daughter and me, Dr. Gould," Christa chipped in. "We look about the same age, don't we? About, say, forty-five, maybe forty-eight?"

Clara smiled. "I'm fifty-two and my mum is sixty-eight! And why? Because we've been following the springs since the sixties. In 1962 I started drinking from the vials stored in the vaults by the SS during the 1943 Lebensborn project. My mother shared this wonderful secret with me."

"Well, I had to. It would be silly to cover up why a daughter would look older than her mother by years, right?" Christa laughed. Clara chuckled with her, slapping her on the hand again as they did that first day in the main building's kitchen.

"So when the vials ran dry, we naturally started eliminating the competition and keeping most of the containers for our own preservation," Christa revealed. "But...then we found out about this fountain in the old Norman fortress occupied by Prof. Ebner, also former Waffen-SS and excellent scientist. He'd also been a part of the Lebensborn project, but not paternally. He was helping the program by adopting one of the children born from the project.

"Mrs. Patterson," Nina said.

"Correct. I had to find a way to own this building and all its...benefits," she smiled, "so I married the heir, my beloved hubby you so love to impress and wrap around that little Scottish finger of yours."

"So we used the fountain in the courtyard," Clara said.

"Until our hold on it was threatened by a potential buyer for the property, one Mrs. Cotswald."

"Oh my God!" Christa agreed with her daughter's eye-rolling recollection. "Mrs. Cotswald! What a clingy, thick-skinned cow *that* was!" The two women flanked Nina's suffering body as they chatted on like a bunch of scone-eating hens at a luncheon, having no regard for her pain or the reprehensible nature of the current circumstances.

"She would just not take 'no' for an answer, would she?" Clara said to Christa as they raved about the annoying woman they'd encountered. Nina could not believe how nonchalant they were about everything, but then again, such was the very essence of a psychopathic nature.

"We found out that she, too, was the result of a Lebensborn pact and that she was looking for her daughters. But we knew what she was looking for, because she was decades younger than her identity document said. So we obstructed the sale by intercepting the mail, among other things, until finally Daniel decided to keep the academy." Christa sighed happily.

"What happened to her?" Nina asked.

"After she finally left Daniel alone, she went to some island somewhere reputed to have an underground river like the one we had here," Clara said.

"While she was there, I was kind enough to invite her husband to teach here on retainer," Christa grinned proudly. "Without him she would have no reason to try again. After she returned from her island getaway she found that she was a widow."

PRESTON WILLIAM CHILD

"Pity. Pity," Clara's meanness seeped through, proving beyond a doubt what fabric she was cut from. "She came back without having found her fountain...*or* her daughters! Talk about shitty luck, eh?"

"This is fucking twisted," Nina murmured, wiping the grins from their aging faces in an instant. "But how is my blood going to help you? I've never even been to a hot spa, let alone bathed in a fountain of youth!"

"Ha!" Christa exclaimed. "My sweetheart! You are the ultimate vial of youth, a human container of the most precious Nazi blood ever engineered for longevity, resilience, and regeneration!"

"Really?" Nina scowled, raising her voice. "Then how the fuck could I contract lung cancer, ladies? Maybe you should do a blood test before you decide to steal the merchandise next time."

"You don't have cancer," Clara denied, looking shocked.

"Clara," Christa seethed, her flaming eyes demanding an explanation very quickly.

"No! No, she's bullshitting us. Naturally. She would say anything to get us to stop draining her fucking blood out! Can't you see what she's trying to do?" Clara defended frantically. Her face was visibly paler after Nina's exposition, even under the overpowering white lights.

"You said she had Lita Røderick's blood from a transfusion four years ago, Clara!" Christa screamed, red in the face.

"She does! It was on her chart when the Order intercepted her blood work after she came back from Chernobyl. Everyone in the Order knew that she'd received Lita's blood

194

just before Lita disappeared. Dr. Cait swore that Dr. Gould was a carrier of Lita's DNA, the exact same composition as Himmler had originally engineered Lita with as *Wunderwaffe*!"

"Jesus Christ!" Nina gasped. "*That* is what this is all about? That red-haired harlot the Black Sun put their hopes on before we watched her get her ass kicked?"

Christa walloped Nina right across the face. Her hand burned into Nina's jaw and cheek, but Nina didn't care. Dr. Cait had betrayed her! She'd believed all along that he was treating her for radiation poisoning, when all the while he'd had some nefarious agenda!

Now that she knew their secrets, she knew how to get under their skins. Nina had always hated the thought of knowing that the blood of Lita Røderick – the monstrous genius genetically produced by Himmler's scientists during World War II – was running through her veins. The evil redhead had almost destroyed her and her friends when they'd raced to find the historical Hall of Valhalla.

"She was not a wonder weapon," Nina laughed coarsely. "Lita Røderick was nothing more than a deformed product of SS-buggery with a tail like a lizard. She was killed by a motorcycle gang inside the meeting hall of Odin, you imbeciles!"

"Shut up!" Christa grunted. She quickly gagged Nina and hushed Clara. "Someone is coming!"

24

"*I*'ll find her," Purdue said urgently.

"You're still under suspicion for Reusch's murder, Mr. Purdue," Campbell said. "I'd advise you to give me her location so that I can send the local police in her area out to pick her up."

"Fine, fine," Purdue replied as he rummaged through his drawers for a thin, rectangular wooden box which he promptly pulled out from under a crow's nest of wiring and switches. Fascinated, Campbell sat watching the frantic genius. It would appear that Dr. Gould was very important to him.

"What the hell is that?" Campbell asked as Purdue unlocked the box and set down the contents on the desk next to his tablet. "It looks like something out of a Sci-Fi movie."

Purdue smiled. "It is. This is a tracking device based on biometrics, the application of recognition analysis based on biological data."

"Facial recognition?" the officer asked, shifting closer with his chair. His curiosity and interest pleased Purdue. Most people just naïvely shook their heads at his remarkable creations, but Campbell asked questions and looked impressed with the intimidating technology.

Purdue hooked up the black and chrome casing to his tablet, expanding the space between his index finger and thumb.

"Fuck me!" Campbell exclaimed as he watched the hardware expand with Purdue's dragging fingers. "How in God's name?"

Purdue chuckled, "Well, the Bible does state that everything is possible through God, my friend. But this makes you think twice about what God really is, hey?"

"Valid point," the stunned investigator admitted. "So where are the scanners that are supposed to have registered Dr. Gould's facial features?"

"Satellite surveillance, Lieutenant Campbell," Purdue said. "There are cameras everywhere, as you know, most of which we might construe as common CCTV surveillance or traffic radar devices. However, many of those are, in fact, government owned, streaming information to large data vaults where information is gathered on the world citizens."

"That sounds a tad paranoid; a bit conspiracy theory-based," Campbell said, wincing.

"I understand, Lieutenant. That kind of dismissive behavior is exactly what they rely on to keep invading privacy, but," he winked at the officer, "if I can track Nina via one of these devices I will have proved to you that this is not a conspiracy theory, right?"

"I suppose," Campbell said in awe. "But why don't you distribute this kind of technology, Mr. Purdue? You could make a fortune with this kind of genius design. I mean, you could be..." he stopped, realizing that he was sitting in an opulent mansion on a historical property, previously owned by kings, "...a billionaire."

Purdue had to laugh at the cop's stupid expression, feeling sheepish about his ridiculous remark. Inside the chrome frame the black screen split into two parts. One lit up with satellite views of various continents, while the other section waited for Purdue to import a passport picture of Nina Gould to work from.

"I'm stumped, Mr. Purdue. Do you have any idea how this device could help us locate criminals?" he mused, looking at the sweating face of his host, concentrating on locating Nina on the landmass of the British Isles.

"I realize that, Lieutenant," he replied while keeping his eyes nailed to the search on the screen. "But you also have to consider the paramount abilities of criminal organizations to duplicate this kind of technology. And should they be introduced to this paradigm, they could find people in Witness Protection, for instance. They could locate politicians, informants, and spies that might be pivotal to trials or important information."

The police officer had to concede that it would be a gamble to release the blueprint of such equipment to the world.

"You see, Lieutenant, the world is not ready for intelligent knowledge. The Human Race is far too primitive to responsibly apply this level of knowledge, and I dare admit, we have an innate insidiousness to test the dark sides of everything intended for good. We, as scientists and teachers, inventors and enforcers of law, cannot allow our efficiency and progressive nature to be jeopardized by the lesser minds of the average human," Purdue presented, finally meeting eyes with his guest. He shrugged, "I realize how egocentric that sounds and I make no excuses for it, because the state of the world these days – and always through history – has proven mankind to be greedy, evil Neanderthals on some power trip. I will never allow my technological talents to be undermined and corrupted by people like those."

"Again, I have to agree with you. Maybe you can play consultant for people like me in extreme cases. I will get the information from you and in turn your technological secrets will be safe. Hey, what say you?" then investigator chuckled, patting Purdue on the back.

"Absolutely! If you happen to find me home. I do have itchy footsteps," Purdue said with a smile, referring to his love of exploration and travel.

"Hopefully not too itchy," Lieutenant Campbell said. "How long does this scanning take?"

"I've only used it once before, in fact. And that was to test the device by looking for my butler when I sent him out for a drive," Purdue said. "But that was area-specific. Now I have to run the whole of England, starting at Hampshire, if that was where she was supposed to have gone. That should take several hours...maybe days."

"Will you please phone me the moment you find out where she is?" Campbell requested. "We'll get her to safety until this Guterman character is safely in Interpol's custody. Of course, if you could use this gadget to find *him*, we would be eternally grateful," Lieutenant Campbell hinted.

"Of course. As soon as I get a result here I'll call you, Lieutenant. Will Melissa Argyle's testimony liberate me from suspicion?" Purdue asked, still floored by the phenomenon of the young woman he thought he knew.

"Yes, Mr. Purdue. But first we have to get her confession signed and get her statement on video. Anything short of that will still be too shaky to build a good defense case on," the officer warned.

"So, I should keep my lawyers ready, then?" Purdue asked, even though he knew the answer.

"For now. Don't leave town. We don't need you to help them make you look suspicious, you know?" Campbell advised.

He left shortly afterwards. On his bare feet Purdue skipped across the smooth, mirror-clean floor of the lobby and vanished down the stairs to his laboratory again, locking the door behind him. With all the analytical data he had accumulated from his underground scientific colleagues he hoped that he would have sufficient knowledge to devise a chamber to attempt reversing time, pushing the envelope of even his abilities. He gathered up cylinders and a small, handheld capacitor with which he was going to store the charge he would need to apply.

Charles came down to the lab, announcing that a package had arrived from Sam containing a water sample. "Sir, Mr. Cleave is on Skype. He says it is imperative that you have him on the line while you open the sample."

"Now?" Purdue gasped. "I don't really have time for this."

"He sounded terribly excited, sir. He said it was about *'that way those people stay young'*?" Charles frowned.

Purdue was confused. With his mind racing around having to escape British air space, curing Nina, keeping Campbell fooled, and the guilt of causing Nina's malady, it was pretty difficult to keep his ducks in a row about a phrase between him and Sam. Then he recalled the e-mail with the pictures Sam had sent him, remarking about how young the locals seem to be for their ages.

"Oh, yes, of course," he sang as it came back to him. "Yes, I would want to talk about that. I shall contact him shortly, but..." Purdue closed the door and turned to his butler. "Charles, I need you to go above and beyond."

"Of course, sir. What do you need?" Charles asked with a nod, his rigid body practically standing at attention. Although his day had been horrible thus far and he direly wanted to take rest in his private life, the fact that his reputation with his boss had been redeemed had vastly improved his demeanor.

"I'm going to look for Nina," he told Charles. "When I find her I'm going to get her out of the country, maybe take her to Sam until I have shaken this murder charge. At least there she'll be safe."

"If I may, sir," Charles questioned the plan. "How do you plan to locate Dr. Gould while the scanner is still running, sir? And what do you need from me?"

Purdue smiled. He looked as exhausted as he was, but somewhere in his face the old cheerful genius had resurfaced, again having a zest for action. Charles could see that his master had regained his confidence and the butler was elated at the welcome change.

"The scanner located her several minutes before Campbell left, but I didn't tell him. I know where she is," he grinned happily. Then he stepped closer to his butler and laid a hand on the man's shoulder, whispering, "What I need you to do, my good man, is to stall the police. They have to believe I'm still here, you see?"

Charles looked at Purdue with concern. "Sir, I don't have to tell you that if they find out you left the country you will be in deep trouble."

"You're right, old boy," Purdue said. "You don't have to tell me."

Charles just smiled, clearly, as always, willing to play along. "Very well, sir."

With that Purdue let his butler out and returned to preparing the instruments he would need to try and help Nina reduce the effects of her illness until he could come up with a more permanent solution.

"Sam!" he exclaimed as Sam's wayward looking image appeared on his monitor. Behind the journalist the skies looked gray and cold as the gusts messed up his dark, longish tresses.

"Aye, thanks for calling, Purdue," Sam shouted over the speaker, hindered by the wailing wind. "Sorry about the connection, but the weather is wild here. Did you get the sample?"

"Just arrived," Purdue said. "Shall I remove it now?"

"Aye, please do. I need you to analyze this liquid and what causes the colors in it," Sam requested. "Around here that water impairs aging, if that is possible without, you know, a balanced diet and regular exercise."

Purdue lifted the plain water bottle from the box with a dismissive smirk, "Perrier, Sam?"

"That's just the bottle we scooped it in," Sam replied. "Can you tell us what's in it, because this bloke here," Sam grabbed old Gunnar and pulled him into the frame with him for Purdue to see, "is...wait, guess how old he is."

Purdue shrugged, trying not to offend, "Um, well, the reception here is not grand, but I'd say the man is in his early sixties?"

"Ha!" Sam exclaimed excitedly, giving Gunnar a high-five before letting the man go back to the fire where he was grilling fish. "Purdue, that bloke is eighty-five years old! Eighty-five!"

Purdue was amazed. He lifted the water bottle to the light, but it looked like average water. "I don't understand. You mean, he drank this very water?"

"No, he bathed in it," Sam beamed, "back in 1969! Look at him! This water practically, well, it seems to slow down time or something."

"Sam, water cannot slow down time, just motion," Purdue negated what he hoped was true.

"Do you me need to call Gunnar over here again? Did you see that? I even checked his I.D. He was born in 1930!" Sam smiled and glanced back at the people behind him before lowering his voice to the laptop. "And this is our secret, alright? This can never get out, alright Purdue?"

"It will not," Purdue said seriously. He looked at the water and though it contained no colors as Sam had mentioned, he knew Sam's word was ironclad. An idea formed in Purdue's head that could solve a lot of problems for a lot of people. "Sam," he said as he grabbed a pen and paper. "Where exactly are you?"

He did not care how furious Nina was with him or how she did not want to see him. There would be plenty of time to hate him once she was well enough.

25

Mrs. Cotswald was as pleasant as she'd been back in the 1980s when she'd last tried to make Daniel Patterson an offer on St. Vincent's. A private seller, she'd had no need of addressing Dean Patterson through estate agencies and high-end commission-hounds. Only her personal lawyer would manage the transfers and her accountant would facilitate the payment from her trust to the Ebner Family Trust of which Dean Patterson and his mother were beneficiaries.

The last time that she'd tried to buy the academy, then little more than a modest ruin with a few lecture halls and one hostel, her purchase had not been approved. Through many months of toiling between agents, attorneys, and third party buyers the Dean eventually elected to keep the property that had been passed down to his mother and himself.

There was never any reason given by his mother why she'd revoked his rights to make singular decisions on the sale of the premises, but he'd accepted it. He knew his mother as the sweetest and smartest businesswoman, therefore, if she took the reins he was okay with it. Little had been revealed about his wife or her life before they met.

Daniel had stayed out of her business out of respect. However, he quickly learned that his wife was as stubborn about her past as his mother had been. When he'd wanted her to help him find out who his mother's birth parents were, she'd refused to 'meddle in Prof. Ebner's affairs,' as she put it. Eventually Daniel had had to abandon the surprise he'd wanted to give his mother on her birthday. This time, he hoped that selling the property that had been taxing on his mother for all these decades would be a positive change, both for her and for him.

"As glorious as ever," he said, smiling as Mrs. Cotswald entered his office. By his remark he was not being flippant at all. The graceful lady still looked youthfully middle-aged and beautiful. Her full hair was tied in a fancy bun and her suit fitted her well-lined figure perfectly. The only indications of aging were her shoes and her spectacles. More comfortable than her usual heeled shoes and boots, she now wore flatter shoes to accommodate her slight limp, and her contact lenses were replaced by thin-framed glasses.

"Dean Patterson, what a refined, old master you have become! How have you been?" she said kindly, smiling and holding out both hands to capture his.

"I'm well. Thank you, Mrs. Cotswald," he replied with a smile. "Hideous weather, I'm afraid. But always lovely to see a sunray during a storm."

"My goodness, Daniel, if you were just a few decades younger," she played, grateful for his charm. With a kiss to the cheek the two decided to discuss business while Daniel accompanied the college's prospective buyer through the hallways, although the gardens would be inaccessible under the angry lightning.

Neither of them trusted the ears walls tended to have, especially in the way their last transaction had been thwarted by details the two of them had discussed alone in Daniel's office. Both parties wanted to avoid that happening again. Their footfalls clapped on the wooden floor that lined the corridor running across the ground floor and over the basement chamber where the archives were kept.

"How's your mother doing?" she asked. "I remember those dumplings of hers! To die for!" She clasped her hands together as the thunder howled, sounding like a pile of boulders rolling across Hook as they ascended the steps to the first floor.

"She is doing well, thank you. Maybe we'll run into her here somewhere. She's always up to something somewhere, like a curious child," Daniel chuckled. "So, now that we're together again, Mrs. Cotswald, and know each other a bit better, I've been meaning to ask you something for some time," he cleared his throat. "Why are you so insistent on this particular property. Is it because your husband is a historian and loves the past of this old place?"

His questions were innocent enough, but they had a deeper, serrated blade attached for the receiving end of his curiosity that Daniel had not intended. A little taken aback, Mrs. Cotswald turned to face him on the first floor hallway that ran along the open balcony overlooking the courtyard.

"My God, Daniel!" She exhaled hard, but she kept her voice away from unintended earshot. "Do you think he came home? My husband has been missing since he came to teach here," she revealed in amazement. "He's never returned to me. Not even after he was dismissed from St. Vincent's."

Daniel frowned as the cool spray pelted the side of his face, but it was not the English weather that left him frozen. "Excuse me? Dr. Cotswald was never dismissed. We assumed that he simply left because of the stress he was under or the personal problems he must have harbored. My God, do you mean to tell me that he is still missing after all this time?"

"Presumed dead," she said plainly, looking out over the courtyard. Her eyes were fixed upon the old fountain obscured by the dancing tree branches. "Of course, I'm not presuming. I know."

"You mustn't think that way, Mrs. Cotswald," he started, but she soon halted his sympathy to enlighten him.

"Daniel, my husband was killed when he discovered the spring of that fountain," she grunted with her face near his in order to keep the conversation in tight quarters. "I know this, because he told me on the phone the night before he disappeared. Dittmar's contract here was only three months in and all had gone well...until he discovered the spring that fountain ran from. Suddenly Dr. Smith insisted he leave and when he would not, she made him an offer of a sum of money to make him leave and terminate his contract. But he refused, asking to complete his contract. The next day..." She shrugged.

"He was just...gone. I thought he'd left overnight," Daniel confessed. "My God, he never made it home? And you think my wife is involved? Mrs. Cotswald, I'm sorry, but all that over an old fountain? That is a bit absurd, even for my wife."

"I don't care about that fountain anymore, Dean Patterson. I did once and so did my husband, but he's gone and I'm tired. There's so much about the world you don't know, my dear. All I want to do now is purchase the place where my husband died, where my daughters grew up, and just live out my days," she said in a voice far older than the woman it came from. She sounded truly tired.

Daniel looked over to the cottages, wondering who the man was speaking to his mother where she was sitting on Dr. Gould's porch. "Excuse me for a moment please, Mrs. Cotswald."

He hastened to the cottages where visiting faculty was hosted. Traversing the courtyard, he passed the suddenly significant stone antique. Even with the holey canopy of the overreaching trees the rain came pouring down on him, rendering his feet unsteady upon the rocky and uneven pathway.

"Mum!" he called out ahead to get her attention, and to get a good look at the man with her. Mrs. Patterson and the man turned to face him just as he made it onto the lawn just short of Nina's porch. Daniel stopped in his tracks and started walking casually up the stairs when he recognized the man. "David Purdue?"

"Yes, he is here to visit Dr. Gould, but he wants to surprise her, so better not tell her until she sees him here," Mrs. Patterson smiled.

"Oh, well, welcome to our humble academy, Mr. Purdue," Daniel wheezed. "Mr. Purdue is one of St. Vincent's biggest contributors, mother. Kept us afloat even in the skinny years."

"You're welcome, Dean Patterson. I trust things are going swimmingly for you and the faculty?" Purdue asked cordially. To his side he could hear Mrs. Patterson snigger, but decided to ignore it.

"Very well, yes, thank you," Daniel said, smiling and shaking Purdue's hand. "I had no idea you knew Dr. Gould. Small world."

"Smaller than you think," his mother said loud enough to herself to make sure they overheard.

Purdue chuckled. "I thought that was why you invited her to teach here, because of her affiliation with me?"

"No, my wife is responsible for inviting Dr. Gould. Dr. Christa Smith, department head," he said proudly.

"Can't say I've heard of her," Purdue said thoughtfully, "but that doesn't mean anything. Just because I move in academic circles doesn't mean that I know everyone."

"Who's that up there? My eyes are not what they used to be," Mrs. Patterson asked, shielding her eyes with her hand and looking up at the balcony.

"Oh, shit! I forgot about Mrs. Cotswald!" he exclaimed. "Please excuse me, Mr. Purdue. I have to conclude my business."

"Certainly," Purdue replied, and watched the Dean run back into the rain again.

"Feisty and zealous, that man," Purdue remarked to Mrs. Patterson. "Does he take after his mother, then?"

Mrs. Patterson laughed, "I hope so. My side of the family has always been very young at heart...and not too clumsy in age either."

MRS. COTSWALD PACED across the wet corridor as she waited for Dean Patterson to return, thanking her lucky stars that she'd invested in shoes that did not torture her ankles. Elated to hear some movement downstairs, she descended to the ground floor where the landing continued on into another landing that led to a level below. Intrigued, Mrs. Cotswald peeked over the wrought iron balustrade, but was disappointed to see that the stairs dropped into a closed trapdoor.

A yelp of fear escaped her at the sight of the dead-end stairs that no doubt led down to some sort of dungeon or torture room, the product of her abusive history along with her creative imagination. Looking around her, she found that nobody was present and her curiosity beckoned.

As softly as she could, Mrs. Cotswald carefully took each step down, but no matter how gently she stepped, the iron would sound her approach like a gallows bell. Before she could make it to the third step from the top landing the trapdoor sprang open. Both the two women emerging, as well as the curious visitor shrieked in woeful surprise.

"Mrs. Cotswald?" Clara asked as Christa peeked past her bottom to see.

"What a surprise!" Christa remarked. "To what do we owe this tremendous pleasure?"

"I was waiting for Dean Patterson and thought to explore a bit," replied Mrs. Cotswald, smiling.

"You shouldn't explore around here," Christa warned. "The wet cold and the eroded old stairs are dangerous if you don't know your way." She finally stepped onto the ground floor landing and smiled at Mrs. Cotswald. "You could catch your death here."

Wishful thinking, you devious bitch, Mrs. Cotswald thought as she read the deceit in Christa Smith's eyes.

"Ah, there you are!" Dean Patterson cried as he jogged closer, soaked and trying to catch his breath.

"Darling! What on earth did you do to get so wet? You'll get sick," Christa moaned, removing her cardigan to drape it protectively over his shoulders.

"I was just checking on my mother," he panted.

Christa uttered an insensitive scoff, "You shouldn't be such a mama's boy, Daniel. She's made it this far in life; she doesn't need protection."

"No, it's not that. She was with a stranger," he smiled cordially, "who turned out to be the great David Purdue! Can you fathom? Lovely having such a famous explorer and an old friend of St. Vincent's visiting us at the same time."

"Why is Mr. Purdue gracing us with his presence?" Christa asked.

Removing his glasses to dry them, Dean Patterson smiled as he said, "Oh, he is here to surprise Dr. Gould."

Clara stiffened, but Christa's hand found hers surreptitiously and squeezed it.

26

*M*rs. Patterson waited with Purdue, but they decided to go and look for Nina when it started to loom towards the evening darkening of the sky.

"Wonder where that darling child is? Usually she naps around 4 p.m. and I bring her dinner around 6 p.m. almost every day. This is the first time that she's been this late," Mrs. Patterson told Purdue. He didn't like it one bit, but he didn't want to jump to conclusions too soon.

"Maybe she's finishing up some marking or making copies, or whatever it is lecturers do at smaller institutions," he speculated. But in his gut he could feel that something was wrong. After Lieutenant Campbell shared with him that the Order was on Nina's trail because of her blood work, he half expected her to be the target of some abductor sooner than later.

Purdue had tried umpteen times to reach her by cell and by e-mail without success. This he'd expected, what with their shaky relationship and her need for space. But when Sam had told him not even *he* had access to her, Purdue knew that the ailing historian was hell-bent on disappearing. But now he at least knew *why* she was being so distant, though it wasn't much of a consolation.

"Should we go and look for her, perhaps?" Mrs. Patterson asked Purdue out of the blue. "I don't know about you, but I don't like this one bit. The poor woman is sick as a dog, smokes herself to death, and is a creature of habit. Who knows where she could be?"

"I concur, Mrs. Patterson," he said firmly. "You seem to have a gut for trouble, as do I."

She chuckled as she opened up her brolly. "My boy, if you only knew my aptitude for smelling trouble, you would make me your bodyguard. Come. We'll start at the archive room where she works when she's not teaching."

With Purdue's lanky body bent to share Mrs. Patterson's umbrella, they traversed the beautiful garden through the threatening weather to see what was keeping Nina at this hour. When they arrived at the plummeting stairwell the trapdoor was open, as it always had been.

"She works down there?" Purdue asked.

"Yes, my dear," Mrs. Patterson said.

"Odd," he replied. "She's terrified of small spaces." He dipped his head under the ceiling as he came down the stairs. Somewhere in his Nazi-weakened trust Purdue was wondering if the nice old lady was leading him into a trap, only to have the trapdoor slammed behind him. But his paranoia was unfounded. She was right on his heel, calling for Dr. Gould into the pitch darkness.

"Wait, Mr. Purdue," she whispered. "There is a light switch here."

A click disappointed their expectations, but ignited their concerns. "Why are we looking for Nina in a dark room, Mrs. Patterson? It's not like she would be sitting in the dark, would she?"

"No, that would be stupid of us. I just thought that she could be lying on the floor, passed out or something. That lady is very ill, you know," the elderly woman told Purdue. "Nose-bleeds and headaches, nausea and fainting spells plague her daily. It's conceivable that she could be lying in the dark."

"I see," he said, fumbling for his tablet. Part of the device contained a sharp LED light.

"What's going on here?" Christa asked from above them. "You will break your necks down there in the dark. The lightning blew the wiring on this grid."

"We're looking for Dr. Gould," Purdue explained, patiently returning up the steps behind the Dean's mother. He had no idea that he was leaving Nina behind in her slow acting coffin, unable to scream from behind centuries of thick stone.

"Nina went to see her specialist in Wolverhampton for tests," Christa informed them with a splendidly played nonchalance. "She took the short break of the public holiday to get her treatment done. Apparently the poor thing has been really under the weather."

"Oh, damn," Purdue sighed. "Would you know the name of her doctor there, Dr. Smith?"

PRESTON WILLIAM CHILD

"No, I'm afraid she didn't say, Mr. Purdue. But I'm sure she should be back by next week. In the meanwhile, would you like to stay for dinner?" Christa invited pleasantly.

"I would rather just get on to Wolverhampton, thank you Dr. Smith," Purdue gave her a cordial nod and smiled.

"No, you won't," she insisted. "There is no way the Patterson's will allow a guest to drive in this hellish storm. Absolutely not. And you can stay for the two days until she returns."

"That is awfully kind," Purdue replied. "I would hate to impose. And I am unannounced too."

"Rubbish," she said, and gave Purdue a wink. "After all, we're already preparing a dinner for Mrs. Cotswald too, so you will not be imposing at all. We have more than enough."

Mrs. Patterson watched her daughter-in-law pretend to be a human. It was chilling to see. But she was not about to embarrass her son by calling out his callous wife again. Not tonight.

IN THE MAIN building's cozy ballroom, the dinner table was decked out and the guests the residents gathered with wine and eclectic cuisine. Mrs. Patterson took her place next to Purdue, while Mrs. Cotswald sat across from them along the dining table. Their hosts sat at the heads of the table, and Mrs. Clara Rutherford was seated at Christa's right.

Christa smiled as her husband chatted as he poured the drinks, keeping her eyes on the interesting field of play before her. One by one she surveyed them.

Look at them, all gathered at my table. Three widows, Christa thought. *The billionaire genius who donates towards Daniel's beloved academy, oblivious to the betrayal of his own medical staff who sent the woman he loves straight into the claws of the Black Sun organization to be used as an incubator.*

Purdue looked a bit tense, not the usual flamboyant extrovert his reputation dictated. Christa figured he was just feeling out among all the strangers. *Probably worried about his stubborn little bitch,* she sneered. Then her eyes fell on some of the others. *Oh, sweet, tenacious Mrs. Cotswald, the idiot who can't tell when she's unwanted. Probably the reason she got the shit beat out of her by Raymond all those years before she married the corpse in the archive room.*

"Happy, deary?" Mrs. Patterson asked loudly, her remark drawing all eyes towards the smiling Christa. She hadn't realized that her self-perceived superiority was showing on her face.

"Oh, um, yes, thank you, Anna," Christa said amicably, successfully fooling all the others that she was smiling with affection. As soon as they'd all returned to their conversations she continued taking stock. *And let us not forget the matriarch, Anna Patterson, bred by SS and turned traitor. Adoptive daughter of Prof. Ebner's good graces, having been raised by one of the Order's finest scientists and now? You've chosen to turn your back on us and you're now only alive because I need your son to manage your estate when I kill you.'*

Christa's black heart throbbed eagerly as her victorious disdain escalated. In fact, had she not been so desperate to tap Nina Gould's precious blood over three days or more, she could have wiped the slate clean of the smaller vermin she was beholding. Purdue's nosy prying to find Nina and

Mrs. Cotswald's annoying recurrence blighting Christa's harvesting of Gould's powerful sanguine elixir made them both intolerable obstacles she had to bear with. Daniel seemed ignorant of his wife's doings. To him, her meetings and clandestine projects were much like a book club, a hobby to keep her busy when she wasn't working – something to help her forge alliances with other women. He was almost correct in that assumption, barring the murderous tendencies when she did not get her way.

Now and then she would exchange looks with Clara, both hoping to maintain the charade until the others retreated to their respective corners and they could check on the progress of Nina's exsanguination. Christa wondered what Daniel would do if he knew that Clara was in fact her child. How would he react if he knew that St. Vincent's administration manager was, in reality, the product of Christa's involvement with one SS-Oberstrumbannführer Martin Hertz for the Lebensborn project?

He knew about her fetish for the antique font in the garden. She'd had an obsession with the moss-covered stone ornament that used to tap the underground river that had now run dry, but Daniel would never believe such nonsense as that of it being a Fountain of Youth. All he knew was that the water spring was one of the reasons he hadn't sold the property before, because his wife loved it so much. Nowadays she didn't even look at it, and yet she still fought to keep the fortress. Why, he did not know.

"Mrs. Cotswald, you told me you've been looking for your daughters all your life. May I ask how you lost them?" Dean Patterson asked.

She gracefully wiped her mouth and she took a hefty

helping of wine before she replied. "Many years ago, I was a young dancer in Latvia. I belonged to a Ballet Company that toured throughout Europe during…" she stopped. She could hardly share her true age with the people around the table, and mentioning that her tale was set during World War II would have been absurd.

"During?" Purdue asked, eager to hear her story.

"Um, during dark times in Poland, where I come from," she recovered. "As I said, I was a dancer, but a terrible injury sustained on stage one night caused me my career."

"That's terrible," Mrs. Patterson frowned.

Mrs. Cotswald shrugged and sighed sadly, "I was young and I got involved with a…*military man*…with whom I had two children." She told her tale as nonchalantly as she could, trying not to make too much of an impression. "But, of course, he left and I could not care for my girls. Having been dismissed from the ballet company, I'd had to rely on the charity of art lovers and friends to get by. Eventually, I had to give up my baby girls for adoption or see them starve. The adoptive parents kept in touch with me about my children, as long as I never visited them."

"You weren't allowed to let your children know you?" Daniel gasped. "That's barbaric."

"Perfect word, my boy," she replied with a crack in her voice, "Perfect word." Holding out her glass to Daniel for more wine, she cleared her throat and tried not to weep. He obliged gladly and sat down to hear the rest.

"As long as I remained a ghost, they would send me pictures and tell me where the girls were schooled, and so on. But somewhere around 1966 I lost touch. At the time my then husband sent me to a boarding house in Steinhöring. From there I was admitted to a secret mental asylum in Graz, Austria. From then on I couldn't find my daughters again, until I followed the adoption trail to Hampshire," she smiled such hope that Daniel wished he could embrace her. "But the trail ran cold again when Prof. Ebner died."

Clara and Christa looked at one another knowingly. Purdue was touched by Mrs. Cotswald's story, but he could feel that she had omitted the core truth. He planned to extract the actual, although unbelievable, truth from her before the night was over. If she was familiar with these people at St. Vincent's, she would be able to provide him with a little more insight on which of them, if not all of them, could have abducted Nina.

One thing was plain to Purdue. He did not buy the Wolverhampton excuse for a minute and something told him that, if he left here, he would never see Nina alive again.

27

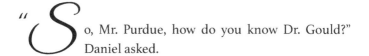o, Mr. Purdue, how do you know Dr. Gould?" Daniel asked.

Christa looked especially interested. Purdue was very well known, both as philanthropist and as explorer and inventor, but Nina Gould did not particularly stand out in academic conversation.

"I've hired her as an historical advisor on several expeditions before," Purdue said. "After so many years of working together we've become firm friends."

"Apparently you've had quite the tiff with some competitors for those relics you love to acquire," Christa mentioned with her mouth full. She washed down her food with some wine and a deadly leer.

"The Order of the Black Sun?" he mentioned deliberately, hoping to start shaking the cage a little. "It's no secret that I've a tendency to get under their skins. But you know, it's all about who is better and faster, I suppose." He laughed, and quickly Daniel laughed with him.

"I thought they were a myth," Daniel told Purdue.

"Oh no, Dean Patterson, they are very much active. In fact, they remind me of a cult of bored college students. Too much money and no productive way to spend their time." Purdue chuckled, intentionally mocking the Order. It worked to his advantage. By using his ability to read faces he could clearly see that Christa Smith was immensely agitated. Regardless, he paid her no attention. Purdue had established where the head of the snake was. All that was left now was finding the sharpest machete to sever that head.

"Maybe they could do more with those relics than to leave them gathering dust in museums," Clara remarked. Purdue marked her too. Christa's shoving foot against hers was too late.

"What Mrs. Rutherford means to say is that some of those artifacts could be used to improve science in this day and age," Christa corrected her daughter, but it was quite redundant.

"That is cause for concern, Dr. Smith. Power should be reserved for those who have the welfare of all in mind, not a minority out to dominate the world with it." Purdue smiled, and raised his glass. "Mrs. Rutherford," he suddenly attended to Clara, "if I may ask, where is Mr. Rutherford?"

"He's dead, Mr. Purdue. He died falling from a cliff while he was on an expedition back in 1987," she recited as if she had been taught the words.

"I'm sorry to hear that," he replied. But he didn't care. Nina was the only thing on his mind and he had to play quickly to find out where she was. What Purdue did notice was the way in which Mrs. Patterson stared at Mrs. Cotswald. The two women looked the same age, both in early their seventies, and now that they sat opposite one another they looked remarkably alike.

"Mrs. Patterson," Purdue addressed the Dean's mother. "How about a turn around the vast dance floor, you and I?"

"Good idea!" Daniel cheered, but the lackluster look on Christa's face denied him the pleasure. He turned his attentions elsewhere. "Mrs. Cotswald?"

"Would love to, but my dancing days ended a long time ago," she smiled regrettably.

Daniel smiled, holding out his hand to Mrs. Cotswald. "No worries, I have two left feet. We can stumble about together." To Christa's dismay they both stood and locked hands to dance. She could feel the property slip out of her hands. She looked at Clara, motioning with her eyes that they should check on Nina.

"Excuse me," Clara said. "I've had too much wine."

Purdue watched her leave, but stayed where he was, intending to trail Christa instead. Also, he had a few questions for Mrs. Patterson. He was hoping that, while he danced with Mrs. Patterson, the music would drown their conversation.

"Are you thinking what I am thinking?" he asked.

"What is that, deary?" Mrs. Patterson asked, pleasantly surprised that he even brought it up and that she was not alone in her thinking.

"Well, Mrs. Cotswald followed the trail of her daughters to this building, to Prof. Ebner, your adoptive father." He shrugged. "Just uncanny, that's all."

"Mr. Purdue, what are you implying?" she asked.

"I think you know, my dear Mrs. Patterson. You were adopted by Prof. Ebner, correct?"

She nodded, so he pried some more. "You lived here when the Cotswalds first tried to buy the property, and you were here when Mr. Cotswald discovered the fountain of youth before he…disappeared. Mrs. Cotswald should have been, if you'll forgive my insensitivity, a name on a mausoleum by now. I can't help but feel that both the spring under the rock fountain and the prospect of finding her daughters here have both had something to do with her wanting this property for so many years."

When he looked down at his dance partner again, tears were trickling from her eyes, glistening in the soft lights of the ballroom. "My son has been trying to find my biological mother for years, Mr. Purdue. But his wife has kept the records from reaching him every time. I think it's because she knows that I…" she hesitated, shooting a glance at Mrs. Cotswald, "am also the product of a Lebensborn union."

Her response confirmed his notion, but he did not fully realize until now that this meant he was surrounded by members of the Order, and not all of them were malicious toward him.

As if Mrs. Patterson knew what he was thinking, she whispered, "Prof. Ebner adopted my sister and I, but he was not a kind man. I suppose that came with the territory of being a

Nazi scientist. You know, he was one of Himmler's finest and pleased the Führer greatly with his discovery of the elixir that could stump aging. Not only would the Lebensborn program deliver strong Aryan stock, but they believed administering the elixir would yield the longevity desired from a super race."

"So you partook in the elixir too?" Purdue asked.

"We had to. But when I learned that my adoptive mother was killed after an altercation with the professor, my sister and I rebelled against him. We refused to be his experiment, especially after the properties of the water he prepared introduced some sort of mild mercury poisoning to our systems. One night my sister pushed him too far and..." she choked, dropping her eyes, "...he drowned her in that very fountain. He punished her. For rejecting his work and refusing to drink that water he simply drowned her in it."

"But he didn't kill you," Purdue said, frowning.

"I lied to him. I pretended to drink from it, leading him to think that his elixir was useless. To him, I was still aging even though I drank of it, rendering his hard work worthless. As a result, feeling that he'd disappointed the Order and the memory of Himmler and the Führer, he shot himself," she said evenly, with not a sign of remorse. "I indirectly caused his death and I inherited this fortress he had turned into an educational institution. And Christa hates that I hold the scepter here."

Purdue was fascinated. Mrs. Patterson did not care about eternal youth or power, the same hunch he'd had about Mrs. Cotswald. It would appear that they really were related if only by their principals. Christa's movement caught his eye. She put down her empty wineglass and stood up when Clara returned. They were discussing something in urgency.

To his disappointment their conversation was quite harmless. Christa turned off the music. "Sorry, everyone. I just want to show our guests to their rooms," she said with a smile. "Clara agreed to give up her room for you, Mrs. Cotswald. If that is alright?"

"That's not necessary," Mrs. Cotswald protested cordially. "I can get a hotel room."

"Rubbish! The Dean and I insist," Christa said smiling. Her husband nodded in agreement.

Purdue waited to hear that he could use Nina's cottage, but instead was offered a room at the Dean's house. It was the ultimate proof that Christa wanted him close to her surveillance and he got the message. Without objection he accepted her invitation, but he would not be kept from snooping. It was not in David Purdue's nature to be denied exploration.

As he was lying on his bed in the third spare room of the Dean's large home, Purdue was checking his tablet, coupled with the device he still had not even named. Using Nina's biometric information, he entered a search in Wolverhampton, just in case Christa, for once, was not lying. His stomach was churning at the thought of her being so very lost, so very untraceable, even more than when she'd first cut communication with him. A morose, emotional void filled Purdue. He could not decide which was worse – losing

Nina forever to death, or knowing that she was alive and well while he was dead to her.

"Nothing," he whispered in the quiet night, after the hosts had retired to bed. "Nothing, nothing, nothing. Wolver-hampton, nothing. Hook, nothing. Nina, where are you?"

His window, and he did check first, was facing out toward the street, away from the courtyard. Christa wanted to make sure that Purdue had no way of investigating while she was asleep. Clara had her own cottage that Purdue did not know the location of, which posed a problem too. An almost inaudible knock at his window coaxed Purdue to take a peek.

Carefully he stole to the window and pulled the drapes aside. He kept his tall frame concealed behind the wall as he did, just in case the barrel of a gun was calling on him on the other side of the window. Instead he found the beck-oning face of Mrs. Patterson standing in her tracksuit and a beanie, giving him a wave to open the window a crack. Through the slit of the frame she slipped him her copy of the house key and whispered, "I'll wait by the door when you're ready."

When he opened the bedroom door, he was confronted with a long, darkened corridor that ran past the open bedroom of the Dean and his wife. Barefoot, Purdue stalked past where he heard the soft snoring of his hosts, wondering if Clara was occupying one of the other rooms tonight. Care-fully he peered around the doorway into the Dean's room and found that two bodies occupied the double bed. Quickly he passed, thankful for the ongoing rainstorm that masked the sounds of his movement.

Barely had he reached the front door when Christa sat up in her bed. Wary of waking her husband, she picked up the phone and called the main building of the academy. Three rings later the phone was answered. Christa's brow darkened as she heard the front door click shut. "They're coming. Get ready."

28

*N*ina fell into darkness more than wakefulness as her body donated her life force to the evil society she was at perpetual war with. The chair was sticky under her buttocks from the involuntary urination that had happened while she'd been unconscious during the first few hours she was held. As her blood became less, her blood pressure dipped dangerously. Hypoxia had already been prevalent before having her blood drawn out of her and Nina's chest was aching far more than the lung cancer could ever batter her with. The lack of oxygen in her system, along with the gradual exsanguination, was draining her of every ounce of energy and rendering her mentally unstable.

During the times she was barely conscious, Nina would talk to herself, but she had no recollection of what she was talking about. Finally, she laughed a lot between *petit mal* seizures and the awful constriction of her clammy skin, the result of her neurological torment. Her senses were going haywire, sending her already frail body into tremors and chills. Nina stared into the darkness where the blurry, flickering lights of the pump were the only sign that she could still see through her failing eyes.

So many regrets filled her as she tried to remember who she was. Nina felt her memories wane as her life slipped away – her name, her origins, her family. Somewhere in between the fleeting images and sour contrition, Nina thought of a man; no, two men.

"Who are you?" she mumbled behind her gag, relieved that she could hear her voice articulating words. It was her way of maintaining her sanity while her body grew heavier and her heart grew tired of trying. "Hey!" she shouted to the two men who kept her company. "I know you, right?" Then she would laugh to convince herself she was happy, only to feel the nausea pressure her. Headaches had become as common as breathing, and Nina's well-groomed nails had broken off in the upholstery of the chair from the spasms of agony that blazed through her veins.

There was a dark-haired man with big dark eyes, wearing a scarf. His hair was wild and sexy, and his voice was clear, but she had no idea what he was saying. Next to him stood a taller man, the antithesis of the other. His hair was white, and behind his glasses his eyes were a piercing blue-green. Nina giggled. "I love you. All of you, I mean, all...both of you...you both..."

She frowned, trying to figure out where she was and why she could see these unknown men while there was no light source around her. Her thigh muscles burned like liquid fire as the male figures looked on. Then they'd be gone, and she would weep tears she did not possess. She was alone, except for the chit-chat of pain.

PURDUE AND MRS. PATTERSON rushed through the rain to get to the main building of the fortress of St. Vincent's Academy. "Mrs. Patterson, wait!" Purdue called softly. "Great Scot, I can't keep up with you. I think your juice is still strong."

Mrs. Patterson had to chuckle at the inferior fitness of the young Scottish man. "Maybe so, deary. I won't be old until they close the lid. Now hurry and keep that crow bar handy. Limber as I might be, I don't have the strength to deliver a good pummeling."

"Right," Purdue replied through wet lips. He tightened his grip on the crow bar the old lady had brought him. "I thought you stayed in the Dean's house, by the way."

She looked horrified. "Och, no! You think I could tolerate that harpy for one single day under the same roof? Hell's bells, no! I live in the aptly named 'granny flat' in their yard."

"And Clara?" he asked. She was his biggest cause for concern; a wildcard that could be anywhere at any time.

"Like Nina she, stays in a cottage on campus grounds. I'm so glad the students have left for the long weekend. My God, she was draining them without keeping track on the amount of energy she took from them," Mrs. Patterson chattered almost non-stop now that she could tell someone outright.

"The students?" Purdue gasped in horror. "Didn't she consider the amount of legal repercussions she could subject the college to?"

"My dear, she is not here for the love of teaching," she said, cocking her head in sarcasm as they made it through an auxiliary entrance to the ground floor interior.

"How does she drain them?" he pressed for information to establish how strong an opponent she would be.

Mrs. Patterson looked up and pointed to the ceiling. "The air-conditioning system, Mr. Purdue." He was astonished at the amount of trouble Dr. Smith had gone to just to stay young and perpetuate her nefarious vampirism. She was way past any affiliation with the Black Sun. In fact, he suspected that Smith had broken away from her duties in the organization when she married into Ebner's family.

"How do you know where Nina is, Mrs. Patterson? It's rather suspect, you understand," he told the elderly lady, who nodded in agreement.

"I heard an ungodly explosion down in the archive room, even above the clapping thunder and the din of the down-pour yesterday," she reported as they neared the stairway to the basement floor. "So I came to investigate."

"An explosion?" he asked.

"It sounded like an earthquake, but it was, in fact, one of the walls in the archive room that collapsed when Dr. Gould accidentally toppled a heavy file cabinet. The impact made the wall give way, so that made a ghastly noise. But when I came to check if Nina was alright, I found Christa and Clara circling the poor girl, toting a bloody Beretta at her!" she said as quietly as she could.

"Good God! Did they shoot her?" Purdue asked with an ashen face.

"No, but I know where they took her," she said seriously.

"Why didn't you interfere then?" he inquired angrily. "Why did you allow them to draw us away earlier when we were right there?"

"David, such a confrontation would have jeopardized the safety of Mrs. Cotswald and yourself, not to mention the fact that she'd kill my son the moment I was out of the way. She wants St. Vincent's, don't you see?" she retorted. "There!" she pointed to the vanishing stairwell.

Reaching the trapdoor, Mrs. Patterson kept watch as Purdue strained to break the lock. It was a hardy, iron contraption that lived up to its name. Purdue took to the hinges instead.

"Clever," Mrs. Patterson remarked.

"Ta," Purdue groaned as he busted the second hinge.

With the thunder roaring every few minutes the two of them descended the stairs into the archive room where Nina had made her office. Purdue used his tablet for light, the strong beam illuminating the dusty tomb of papers and records.

"Oh Jesus!" Purdue exclaimed inadvertently as his light fell on the broken wall and the leering skeleton within. The new air that had been let into the chasm had worked at deteriorating the fine bones and clothing, but Mrs. Patterson recognized the style of clothing as belonging to the historian who attended during the early nineties.

"That's Dr. Dittmar Cotswald, that," she affirmed while Purdue stared.

"Great. But we aren't here to free him. Pray to God that Nina is not in the same condition," he reminded her. "Where is she, Mrs. Patterson?"

"When I was a little girl, Prof. Ebner used to experiment on me and my sister in here," she struggled to say. Before Purdue could reply, she pulled a hidden lever and the wall shifted aside. Cautiously Purdue shone his light into the small tunnel, looking to his partner for encouragement.

"I wish there were a window here. The lightning would have helped much to navigate through here," he whispered. Vaguely he could hear laughing, muffled by fabric or wood. Purdue was not a man of colorful imagination or ghostly affinity, but the prospect of what caused those sounds just creeped him out completely. "Well, we have the right weather for the kind of feelings I'm feeling."

"Yes, I'm scared shitless too, deary," the spirited old lady agreed. She clung to Purdue's arm as they progressed and then whispered, "Okay, soon the room should be on your left."

Purdue lit ahead and there it was, an entrance without any door. The hideous mumbling and laughing were coming from inside. As they drew closer they could perceive the sound of a machine humming while every now and then a *beep* would sound.

What Purdue saw when he turned the corner far surpassed any horror film he could place with the weather. His light fell on Nina, tied to a grotesque chair, her thigh seeping blood that pooled in a dry coppery mess on the chair. Her eyes had gone from bright and brown to bloodshot and milky, staring insanely at him. Pale blue from the cold chamber, her skin exhibited the dead paleness of a cadaver.

"Jesus Christ, no!" Purdue wept instantly, rushing to pluck the needle from her before it could take another ounce from her.

"No!" Mrs. Patterson yelled, grabbing his hand. "If you pull it out she will hemorrhage..."

"She is hemorrhaging *now!*" he screamed at Mrs. Patterson, his wet eyes fuming and hopeless. "I can't let her endure one more second!"

They did not hear Clara sneak up behind them. A thunderous shot echoed through the lower floor as she gunned down Mrs. Patterson. Purdue shouted and lunged forward to punch the gun-wielding woman right in the face. Her nose broke on impact and she fell to the ground, but she tried to shoot again. Purdue kicked the gun from her hand and scooped it up to put in his pocket. Crouching down next to her, he grabbed handful of her hair and hissed, "Get Nina free or I will bash your skull in right here."

"I know you, right?" Nina slurred slowly at Purdue as Clara removed the gag before removing the needle from her thigh. Purdue sobbed, holding the diminished hand of his ex-girlfriend in his, afraid that it would grow limp while he warmed it.

"Yes, you know me," he said, smiling through his tears.

Nina smiled weakly. "Aye. You're *Sam*."

Purdue swallowed hard. His heart broke again, but he had to make sure hers kept going. He growled at Clara. "Give her a transfusion! Put her blood back immediately!"

"I can't do that," Clara started to explain through collapsed nasal cavities, but Purdue dealt her a backhand that sent her reeling.

"Put her blood back!" he shouted, cradling Nina in his arms. "My God, you're so thin," he whispered as her boney body poked his skin. Mrs. Patterson groaned from the corner where she had collapsed.

"It's too late," Mrs. Patterson told Purdue. "Her organs are failing already."

"No! I will fix her. Just give her blood for long enough and I will fix it all," Purdue insisted, his voice twisting in desperation as he laid his face on Nina's chest. There was barely any sign of a heartbeat. "I just need to get you to the Faroe Islands, Nina. They have water there that could cure you, give you back your health, and even keep you young! Just hold on," he cried, "just long enough for me to get you to Sam. He's waiting, do you hear? Sam is waiting for you."

He lifted Nina's small, limp body into his arms and ordered Clara to prepare the machine for transfusion. Mrs. Patterson, having been wounded in the leg, stood up and shoved Clara aside. "The least we can do is try, right?" she told Purdue. "I'm not promising anything, but if we can get a few more pints in she would be able to travel with you."

"Mrs. Patterson, you are a goddess," Purdue sniffed.

"I'm no doctor, but even nurses have a duty to provide medical help," she replied. "Now, get hold of your people on the other side to have a doctor on stand-by at the airport."

Purdue sat next to Nina, using his tablet to contact Sam while Mrs. Patterson attempted to save Nina with what she could find. She was performing her tasks in the very room where Prof. Ebner had subjected her and her sister to his sick experiments, but she did not care. While Purdue conversed hastily with his friend on the screen, Mrs. Patterson was doing a good job of administering the butterfly needle to Nina's flimsy vein. She paid no attention to Clara, who was confined to the shower cubicle where Ebner used to bathe his daughters in pesticides.

29

"Where is he, Jeeves?" Lieutenant Campbell asked the butler.

"Excuse me, sir, but my name is Charles Amberson. Not Jeeves," Charles corrected the investigator.

"Are you being a prick, Charles?" Campbell asked, sounding a lot like Charles' old football pals.

"I believe I am introducing myself, sir," he told Campbell.

"Christ, it's like talking to Mr. Spock. Are you aware that you are obstructing justice by refusing the police access to this mansion?" the lieutenant growled at the front door of Wrichtishousis, where Charles was deterring his entry in the middle of the night.

"No sir," Charles replied. "I am under no obligation to allow access without a warrant."

Lieutenant Campbell realized that his usual intimidating manner was not going to fly this time. The butler was correct and the lieutenant knew that he would not get any help unless he used another approach. And he could freeze to death in the cold night air on top of it.

"Listen, Charles. I understand that you are only doing your job, but I have to impress upon you the ugly repercussions for your boss if he ditches us. All I ask is his whereabouts," Campbell sighed.

"To arrest him?" Charles asked, secretly enjoying his power trip over the cop.

"I can't arrest him yet. We don't have enough evidence to bring him in, you see? You may as well tell me, because he's being targeted by the very people who tried to kill him at the Sinclair Facility. Please, Charles, this is no bullshit. I need to know where David is because they already do. If I can't send Interpol to his location, they'll kill him and walk away," the rugged lieutenant explained with no small measure of shameless pleading.

"Lieutenant Campbell, I will lose my job," Charles persisted.

"Well, when they shoot your boss in the head you'll be out of a job anyway," Campbell said, shrugging. "It looks like you really have no choice, son. We're both on David's side. We have to save Nina Gould and we have to save him and we have to do it before they catch up to them, do you understand the weightiness of this issue?"

Charles sighed and mulled it over. He could feel Lily's eyes burning into his back and he knew that she was easier to crack than he was.

Charles' phone rang.

"Excuse me, sir," he apologized, and answered the phone. It was Purdue.

"Sir, Lieutenant Campbell is here as we speak," he reported with his back to the large investigator in the doorway. Still, Charles kept a keen eye on the unwelcome guest using the mirrors in the lobby. He kept his voice low, but he could tell that Campbell knew who he had on the line. Suddenly the butler looked utterly surprised. "Of course, sir. Please hold."

With the wind properly out of his sails the flabbergasted butler walked over to Campbell and handed him the phone. "It's for you, sir."

Looking as perplexed as the butler, Campbell took the call.

"Purdue?"

Charles waited patiently for his master to complete the call, feeling a right twit. He pretended to look out over the porch furniture while he waited, trying to eavesdrop, but he heard little more than muttering from the police investigator who paced the driveway.

At last the cop came smiling, returning the phone. To Charles' surprise, he was not gloating. Instead he passed it on, "Talk to your boss quick, alright? Hurry, we have plans to make."

"Listen, Charles," Purdue said, "I've asked Campbell to alert Interpol about Guterman. His lackey here is going to let him know that Nina and I will be traveling to the Faroe Islands post haste. We're going to bait her into it."

"Yes, sir."

"I need you to call my flight crew to charter a flight to Vágar Airport, Faroe Islands with my private jet," Purdue instructed as Charles ran into the library room next to the dining hall.

"Sir, just one moment, please. I'm getting a pen and paper," he puffed as his polished Italians clapped on the marble floor. "Right! Faroe Islands airport. Shall I send the jet to collect you at the nearest airfield in Hampshire?"

"No, no, Charles," Purdue rushed. "You know how I always tell you to use initiative?"

"Yes, sir?"

"Today is not that day, alright?" Purdue said hurriedly. "Just take down the information and execute the orders. Just for today."

"Yes, sir."

Campbell smiled as he watched the red-faced youth scribble down what he already knew. He gave the lad a quick wave to announce his departure and hoped he would get the instructions right and not foul it up for everyone involved.

30

---

*P*urdue had made the arrangements, but he was no calmer. Nina was in a bad way, wheezing and shaking, regardless of the blankets they'd covered her with. He was talking in her ear and holding her hand while she slipped in and out of consciousness.

"We can't administer fluids or blood too quickly, Mr. Purdue," Mrs. Patterson advised. "It would be deadlier than her current threats."

She didn't notice the menacing frame of Clara Rutherford stealing towards her from behind, holding an old heart monitor box from Prof. Ebner's collection above her head. With his eyes on Nina, Purdue also did not see her come. As she aimed the steel box at Mrs. Patterson a loud gunshot clapped from nowhere, propelling the assailant backward from the force of the second and third slugs that dissembled Clara's youthful looks in an instant.

Purdue's jaw dropped and a cowering Mrs. Patterson held

onto him for support as Mrs. Cotswald lowered her gun. "Stay away from my daughter, you bitch."

"Mrs. Cotswald? You are a godsend! Holy shit! I can't believe what just happened!" Purdue exclaimed in amazement. It seemed to him that whatever was in the Fountains of Youth not only prolonged youthful regeneration, but also kept courageous attitude intact. "You ladies are something, I tell you that," he huffed, on edge from the whole night's negative excitement.

But the elderly ladies heard nothing. They were locked in embrace, weeping at their strange reunion after a lifetime of being apart. "You know, I've never called anyone 'Mum' before," Mrs. Patterson admitted. "Rather odd to start now, right?"

Mrs. Cotswald, overjoyed at being with one of her daughters again, shook her head and chuckled through the tears. "I've searched for you for so long, my darling. Better late than never!"

"She isn't going to make it, Mr. Purdue," Mrs. Patterson warned. "She's lost too much blood already."

"I will *not* accept that!" he barked. "I will give every drop I have to save her. The cancer she suffers from is *my* doing and I will not let her die!"

"My God, what did they do to you?" Mrs. Cotswald asked the emaciated Nina, who's eyes barely looked at her.

"They harvested...m-my blo—," Nina spoke through arid lips. "Lita's blood..."

"Lita Røderick? You were *the vial* everyone in the Order was speaking of?" Mrs. Cotswald gasped. "*The Vial* is a person? God, that is sick, even for them!"

"The Vial?" Purdue asked.

"In the Order, ever since Hitler promised my dance instructor that I would 'stay pretty forever,' there'd been myths all over the globe about the Fountains of Youth that contained such regenerative properties that those who drank it or bathed in it would defy aging," Mrs. Cotswold explained. "I just never thought they really used *people* to carry the genetically engineered blueprint!"

"Lita?" Purdue reminded her.

The elderly woman looked annoyed. "Lita was a monster, not a person."

"Nina was almost killed while we locked horns with Lita's imps, and that was when they transfused her blood into Nina's body," Purdue filled her in.

"I'd heard the story, but thought it was a farce. Who could believe that there was a Fountain of Youth with blood capable of impeding cell division, in other words, to thwart aging as far as science permitted?" She placed her hand on Nina's clammy forehead and revealed, "You, my dear, are the Fountain of Youth the Order has been referring to."

Purdue was shocked. "But she has cancer. That's all about rapid cell division!"

"Yes, but had she not been The Vial of Life, the Font of Youth, the illness would have spread far quicker. Had she had normal blood, your poor lady friend here would have perished months ago," Mrs. Cotswald clarified. She smiled sweetly and took Mrs. Patterson's hand. "And here I was, looking in all the wrong places for mountain springs and rock fountains all these years, hoping to put a hold on aging until I've seen my beloved daughters."

Nina drew a deep breath and groaned out a few words. "She says we must hurry up because G-Goo...no, Guter-m..."

"Guterman?" Purdue asked quickly.

"Aye," Nina said. "Coming to kill you s-s-soon."

"Who told you that, deary?" Mrs. Patterson asked Nina.

"Gertie. Gertie says...w-we..." Nina passed out.

"Who the hell is Gertie?" Purdue asked, hoping that it was not one more opponent to evade.

Both the old ladies stood dumbstruck, until Mrs. Patterson finally said, "Gertrud was my sister. She drowned in the fountain outside many years ago."

Mrs. Cotswald held back her tears. She hadn't known that her other daughter had died before she could meet her. Mrs. Patterson smiled and held her mother's hand. "Well, it looks like she's still hanging around with us, hey...Mum?"

As if possessed suddenly, Mrs. Cotswald rolled up her sleeves, looking absolutely focused. "Anna, dear, care to run a tab for Dr. Gould from the Bar of Cotswald? I hear the elixir behind that bar is downright surreal."

Purdue cried out an exclamation of joy!

"Coming right up, Dr. Gould," Mrs. Patterson smiled and made haste to get her mother's virtually immortal donation to Nina."

"Don't you have to be the same type?" Purdue panicked.

"Not to worry. The blood used in engineering super soldiers like Lita Røderick came from a single source in 1945. Yours truly," Mrs. Cotswald boasted. "If Lita's blood was flowing in Nina's, it's safe to use mine."

"So you are the original Fountain of Youth," Mrs. Patterson praised her mother.

"I'm very concerned about your injury, Mrs. Patterson," Purdue said.

"It's not near any major arteries, love. First things first, right?" she told the amicable young man.

Nina's eyes fluttered open somewhat a few minutes into the new transfusion. Before her sat a very graceful elderly woman who looked no older than seventy years. Her hair was on her shoulders, lush and shiny gray. She smiled at Nina with big blue eyes. "Feeling better yet?"

"Aye. Thank you so much, ma'am," Nina said, smiling as Purdue wet her lips.

"Call me Ami," the lady said. "But don't thank me yet. You're not out of the woods yet. We're just keeping you ticking so that you can make it to the Faroe Islands."

Nina fell asleep again, unaware that the three people with her were rushing to get her out of there before Guterman and his animals came to assassinate them all.

31

*C*hrista was beyond furious. She'd drugged Daniel and locked him in the house so that he could not get in her way when she and Clara annihilated the snooping buyer and the threat from Edinburgh. When she came calling on Clara in the archive room she'd found it empty, with the secret door open. A sick feeling of defeat crawled over her spine and curled up in her stomach. Christa Smith stopped dead in her tracks when she found the bloody corpse of her daughter, Clara, gunned down by three bullets in strategic places.

But Christa did not weep for her child. She readily became incensed that she'd lost the Vial she'd been trying to locate for so long, her last chance to reclaim her fading youth. Marrying Daniel had yielded nothing but an annoyingly kind husband who worshipped her to boredom. Until he included her in his will as benefactor to inherit St. Vincent's Academy, she could not waste him. What was the point of being married to him if the fountain on his property had run dry? Well, Christa Smith had hoped that digging a little deeper would redeem the former splendor of the stream.

Now she, too, had lost a daughter.

"Anna, I know you sprung that nosy bastard from my guestroom," she sneered out loud under the soothing disturbance of the rain. "And when we catch up, you will not grow a minute older, you old hag!" In Clara's limp hand Christa found her cell phone. By the looks of it Clara had been busy writing a text message to her mother before she perished.

'ANNA COTSW PURDUE *Vial tt Faroes sorryyyyyyyyyyy*'

CHRISTA LOOKED up at her daughter's unrecognizable face as she took her phone. "I'll miss you, sweetie," she said softly, draping one of the operation sheets over her. "At least you were good for something in the end."

She stormed out to her car and in the cracking rumble of the storm made a call to Guterman.

"It's me. Did you take care of Argyle?" she asked.

"Not yet. I'm having her snuffed by a police officer next week when she shows her traitorous face in court," he replied. "But not that I need to explain my plans to the likes of you, Dr. Smith. There are more important issues to be discussed. Is the Vial tapped out?"

"I need you to not freak out. I have a lead," she said.

"A lead to what?" he barked. "I knew you would fuck this up."

Christa took a deep breath. Guterman was not someone to talk back to, even when he was wrong. "Guterman, I know exactly where they are going. Meet me at Farnborough in two hours and bring your passport."

"Where are we going?" he asked, sounding a bit more content.

"I'll meet you when we land there. Your reputation does not allow me to be generous with information," she admitted. "Your pilot will have the coordinates. See you there."

"Smart woman," he approved. "No wonder you've survived the leech pond this long. I'll see you there. And Christa, don't make me wait."

———

WHEN PURDUE's pilot announced that they were entering Faroese air space the billionaire could not help but smile. Nina's pulse was strong and Anna Patterson looked confident that she would make it to Sam's sworn wonder well.

"You think my grandson is safe with that witch?" Ami Cotswald asked.

"I hope so. She won't kill him until he's overwritten my clause in my Testament, Mum," Anna smiled. "Until then, she'll keep him alive. Or until I find a way to kill the cow."

"That wish might come sooner than you think, Mrs. Patterson," Purdue smiled. "Guterman is following us here, and no doubt Christa is accompanying him so that they can tap Nina's blood for good this time."

"How is that a good thing, deary?" Mrs. Patterson asked.

"You'll see," he winked, wiping Nina's face gently with a moist towelette.

AFTER THEY HAD TOUCHED down in Vágar in the dead of night, the crew helped the Faroe Island's ground staff move Nina from the plane to the vehicle that Sam Cleave had arranged.

"Thanks, gentlemen," Sam said to the ground staff after Nina was safely seated between Ami Cotswald and Anna Patterson. He and Purdue exchanged a quick handshake and embrace before the two men got into the front of the vehicle. Ami and Anna were taken by the good-looking men who introduced themselves as Sam and Heri.

"You ready, ladies?" Sam asked.

The naughty Mrs. Patterson was eager to answer, "Oh yes, deary. Please, go ahead and drive us."

Purdue laughed as Sam's face turned red. "Go on, old boy. Time is of the essence."

SHORTLY BEHIND THEM Christa's helicopter landed. She could see Purdue's jet taxi to the bays.

"Get ready," she told her four passengers, Black Sun operatives who were on retainer for unforeseen excursions like these. "We have to swoop down and retrieve the Vial before they know what hit them. In and out! Are we clear?"

Her colleagues cocked their concealed firearms as the helicopter touched down. Briskly they rushed to Purdue's jet to take their places under it. Oddly, there was no ground staff outside and security was wonderfully lenient, taking little notice of the new arrivals. Christa stepped out of the chopper and approached the private jet, eager to load Nina back into her craft and rip Purdue's head off for killing her daughter.

"Excuse me, madam?" a voice said behind her.

"I don't have time," she snapped. "I have to meet those passengers when they disembark."

"I'm afraid you'll have to make time for me," the man insisted. Christa turned to face him, scowling from vexation. "Did Guterman send you?"

"He did. But I haven't seen him here yet, have you?" he asked.

"No, naturally not. I just arrived here, you idiot," she grunted. "Once he arrives you can bring him on board Purdue's jet. That would be this one, right here. Okay?"

Her sarcasm was wasted on the man. Calmly he pointed out, "You will not find them there, Dr. Smith."

She swung around. "Why not?"

"Because they landed in an unmarked plane thirty minutes ago. They've gone."

"Then who is in Purdue's jet?" she shouted, but the shouting of arrest officers soon got her attention as her colleagues were taken down and arrested.

"That would be Interpol, madam," the man affirmed. Christa, seething at Guterman's betrayal, turned to run, but the officer simply grabbed her and cuffed her. "Welcome to Vágar."

32

When the clock struck 2:30 a.m., Johild saw the headlights of her cousin's car appear over the hillock behind the house.

"They're here! Come Papa, we have to hurry!" she whispered as hard as she could to wake her father, who'd been waiting by the kitchen table for Sam Cleave's friends to arrive. He jerked back, waking harshly. "Sorry," she winced. "But come, we have to get Sam's friend to the Empty Hourglass."

Gunnar jumped up and gathered up his car keys and phone. "Is everyone ready?"

"Everyone's ready," she confirmed.

She jumped into the 4x4 with her father and they led the way. The two large vehicles trekked over winding roads and hills that rose and fell in the cold dark that breathed saline air through the slits in the windows.

"Keep her warm, please," Sam said to the ladies in the back.

"Don't worry. She is snug as a bug back here," Ami smiled. "Hold on Dr. Gould. We're almost there."

"Are we?" Purdue asked.

"Yes, it's just a few more kilometers to the north," Ami directed.

Heri's pristine eyes glimmered in the dashboard lights as he peeked in the mirror at the woman in the back. "Have you been here before?"

"A long time ago. I came to look for the Empty Hourglass," she smiled, but Heri and Sam glared at one another in distrust as the lady continued. "I met the sweetest two locals here. Wonderful young men..." her voice cracked. "But it ended in tragedy."

"Why? What happened?" Anna asked.

"I was with bad people who wanted to use the Empty Hourglass for greed and to corrupt the weak even more," she said angrily. "The Empty Hourglass – the name was given by a man called Jon. I never got to know his last name, but that was what he and his brother dubbed it because it had no sands of time."

"Lovely," Anna said, smiling.

"Yes, it was," Ami agreed with a sad smile. "Guterman, the fiend...he killed Jon right in front of me. His brother got away, thank God. But I made sure they never found the place where the two young men found the pool. Even when I returned years later, I never betrayed their secret. I saw Jon's brother, but out of fear that the Order would notice him, I ignored him."

"Lucky for him. You seem to be death on legs," Heri said sharply. "I'm the nephew of those two men. My uncle Gunnar has told us all about you."

Ami did not reply. She could not possibly convey how sorry she was, but Heri had not had enough yet. "Gunnar is in the vehicle ahead of us. I suggest you keep your identity hidden."

"How can she?" Purdue asked. "She has barely aged."

WHEN THEY REACHED the site of the Empty Hourglass, they all braved the ice-cold wind and the darkness to crack open the rock over the pool. Gunnar did the honors, happy to impress the woman he secretly recognized, the one who'd hidden him from discovery so many years ago when the Black Sun's dogs came back. But it was the beautiful woman who resembled her that he was most interested in. "Hello, I'm Gunnar." He smiled and shook her hand.

"Lovely to meet you," she said. "I'm Anna Patterson from England."

"Good to meet you, Anna Patterson from England. Do you have any Viking in you?" he asked.

"Uncle Gunnar!" Heri interrupted and dragged him aside. "Help us lower Dr. Gould into the water."

"Is the pool's water as cold as this bloody ocean air?" Purdue asked.

The locals chuckled. "Fortunately not. It's temperate, from a lava presence deep in the underground caverns," Heri explained.

"Ah," Purdue said, "that would explain the strange properties of the water I analyzed. There seems to be magnetic particles prevalent in the water. They seem to be influenced by the geographical location of the rock. Like the Northern Lights, it's just a magnetic storm of particles differing in intensity, influenced by the stronger polar influence."

"That causes the slowing of age?" Johild asked Purdue.

"In theory, yes. The unnatural application of geomagnetic particles coupled with its influence on the molecular structure of red blood cells has something to do with impairing rapid cell destruction without compromising the natural process of cell division," Purdue explained. He shrugged, "As far as I could gather, anyway."

"Oh my goodness! Isn't that beautiful!" Anna Patterson said in awe of the slowly blossoming colors exuding from the lukewarm water. Apart from the flashlights Sam, Heri and Gunnar held, it was the only illumination of the area. In wonder, Purdue and his elderly accomplices stood staring at the phenomenon.

"It's like a portable Aurora Borealis," Ami jested. "I can't wait to see that young lady catch her breath."

Nina was barely conscious when they brought her to the pool at the convergence of the ruins. The night was black and cold, but she was in so much pain the temperature hardly agitated her. Before Purdue and Heri lowered her into the water chute, she looked at Purdue and whispered with a smile what she hadn't said in the torture chair, "I know you. You are David Purdue."

Purdue only smiled as she went under for a moment to cover her entire body in the dancing colors of the lazily bubbling spring. But behind his smile a warm tranquility took hold of his heart, knowing that Nina had made peace with him at last.

A HAIL of bullets rained down on them from the dark. Johild was struck and she fell to the grass before her cousin could catch her.

"Jo!" Gunnar screamed. He jumped up and raced to his daughter's aid just as a man appeared from the dark, pointing a gun at him. With a grin on his familiar face, Guterman said, "Time to join your brother, boy!"

He pulled the trigger, hitting the woman who jumped to shield him. Heri and Sam tackled Guterman, wrestling the gun from him while Guterman's goons burned up bullets against rocks. So far only Johild and Ami had been hit, but Johild had crawled to where Anna Patterson was holding out her hand.

Nina was drowning in the spring. The surface of the water was too far down from the edge and the shaft too narrow for her to effectively tread water. Purdue's arm came over the edge and grabbed her forearm, just holding her above the surface until the shots ceased. A distance into the darkness many male voices could be heard shouting for help and barking orders.

Anna was compressing Johild's bullet wound behind the rock. Ami Cotswald was lying in Gunnar's arms, barely alive.

Lights came on one by one, surrounding and illuminating Guterman's thugs; then more at a time, until Order's henchmen realized that local fishermen brandishing knives, guns and harpoons surrounded them. They had gathered around the ambush Guterman had planned for Purdue's party, just as Purdue had predicted. He'd told Sam to make sure Nina could be baptized without the danger of being captured again, and between Sam, Heri and Gunnar they had arranged an ambush of an ambush, should there be one.

Gradually they narrowed in closer, but the surrender of foreign devils like Guterman and his men meant nothing to the locals. They'd grown tired of their own constantly being killed for the greed of the Black Sun and its Nazi ideology. Such pursuits for their land's secrets and beauty would end this night.

"What's happening?" Purdue asked Sam.

"Just look away. Tonight it's time for a different kind of whale hunt," Sam advised him.

They both lay on their stomachs with their arms dangling down the shaft to hold Nina up as her body absorbed the miracle elements.

"It tingles," she slurred with a dreamy smile. Her cheeks flushed, even though she was still struggling to breathe. "But it doesn't hurt. Like a hundred fingertips tingling…"

Purdue and Sam smiled at each other, relieved that she was coherent.

"Did they kill anyone?" she asked, barely having enough breath.

Sam looked back to survey the casualties. "I think they killed the limping lady."

"Mrs. Cotswald. She saved my life," Nina wept for the original Vial commissioned by the Order of the Black Sun.

"It looks like she saved another one," Sam reported.

Anna had joined her mother who was lying in Gunnar's arms, while Johild, supported by her cousin, came to Gunnar's side. He was crying for the limping ballerina he'd once known under the darkest of circumstances. She reached up and wiped Gunnar's tears. "Hey, hey," she said through bleeding lips, "now we're even."

"Yes," he laugh-cried, "yes, we're even, dear Ami."

Anna was crying inconsolably when she took her mother's hand. "But I just found you, Mum. You just found me," she sobbed.

Her mother smiled, still. "My darling, the awesome thing is that I did find you! After I thought I never would, I finally know you! How lovely is that?"

Anna tried to smile for her mother. It was the least she could do to make her passing gentle. "It is grand, Mum. It is so grand!"

Just before she closed her eyes Ami looked delighted. Anna had to ask, "What is happening, Mum?"

Ami smiled, "I am dancing again."

END

Made in the USA
Las Vegas, NV
06 July 2021

26008814R00152